Praise for *Roy of the Rovers*

"It has **everything that a football fan needs...** match day action, local club rivalry, modern football politics, trials, crunching tackles, tricks, misses and goals. It also has everything that today's children need as they grow up. It is jam-packed with positive role models, girls involvement in Women's Football, respect, mental well-being, good work ethic, education and aspiration." – *Books for Topics*

"Packs a lot of punch in its short and simple to read pages... **It captures the feel of playing and having a passion for football** at an early age very well. More than that it sets out the stall of the new Roy Race, his family background, his friends and enemies, where he lives and his work ethic." – *Comic Scene Magazine*

"**I give it 5,000,000 stars**! I recommend it to 9+ football fans but also non-football fans. I'm not a football fan but I still really enjoyed reading this book. Look out for the graphic novels and the rest of the series. Amazing!" – *The Book Brothers*

"**Football-lovers will love the description of on-pitch action** which is pacy yet satisfyingly detailed. This is a book that I am looking forward to putting on the shelves at school – I know already that it will be a popular t' 'ootball-loving children ch

First published 2019 by Rebellion Publishing Ltd,
Riverside House, Osney Mead, Oxford, OX2 0ES, UK

ISBN: 978 1 78108 722 0

10 9 8 7 6 5 4 3 2 1

A CIP catalogue record for this book is available
from the British Library.

Printed in Denmark

Creative Director and CEO: Jason Kingsley
Chief Technical Officer: Chris Kinglsey
Head of Publishing: Ben Smith
Editor: Rob Power   Design: Sam Gretton   Cover image: Ben Willsher

Follow us:

royoftheroversofficial royoftheroversofficial royoftherovers

www.royoftherovers.com   info@royoftherovers.com

The story so far...

Roy Race is a totally normal sixteen-year-old; he studies at college, fights with his little sister - and plays centre forward for Melchester Rovers.

Ok, so he's not *that* normal.

And while it might sound like Roy's got the perfect life, he's got a lot on his plate.

He's had to overcome injuries, social media scandals, the perils of fame and the pressure of performing as one of the best young footballers in the country.

Plus, things aren't exactly easy at home. Roy cares for his disabled father, helps his over-worked mother out as much as he can, *and* coaches his little sister Rocky as she attempts to start a football career of her own.

Of course, all of this would be a lot easier if Melchester Rovers were the biggest club in the country.

But they're not.

In fact, the once-mighty Rovers are in League Two, and although Roy and his teammates have managed to save the club's season, now comes the real test: can they make it to the play-off finals and a shot at promotion to League One?

And what will happen to their club - and their football careers - if they don't?

Roy might be the youngest striker in the football league, but he still carries the hopes and dreams of every Rovers fan on his shoulders when he steps on the pitch...

IMAGINE THIS.

You're playing up front for the team you've supported all your life. The striker alongside you is your best friend from school. If you win this game your team will be through to the play-offs, with the chance of promotion and a trip to the National Stadium.

It's the stuff of dreams.

And it happened to Roy Race.

MINUTES INTO THE game – the home fans making so much noise the players couldn't hear each other's calls – a long ball came upfield from the Melchester Rovers keeper, Gordon Stewart.

Blackie Gray – Roy Race's best friend – took the ball and knocked it on to Roy.

Roy read the fall of the ball right and powered into the D on the edge of the penalty area. The ball bounced once, twice, then Roy hit it low and hard. A half-second later it thumped off the post and span out for a goal kick to Holverton Wanderers.

Close.

But not close enough.

Even so, Roy grinned. He stretched his ankle out, put some weight on it. It felt okay. In fact, it felt good. He knew that he had recovered from the ankle injury that had kept him out for weeks. Now, he just had to get over that nagging fear he had every time he ran with the ball. Fear of being fouled. Fear of being injured.

Coach had told him this might happen.

But Roy Race was back all the same.

And just in time. Because there was more to this game than first met the eye. If Melchester beat Holverton Wanderers they would be in the play-off semi-finals vying for promotion to League One. If they didn't, then the football club Roy loved, his local team, might stop playing in Melchester altogether and be moved to another town. And then what would happen to Roy's dream of playing professionally for his beloved Rovers?

Holverton had already been promoted after finishing second in League Two and were playing showboat football now, looking forward to a summer of rest.

Their goal came from nothing.

A quick one-two in the centre circle and

the Holverton winger, Martin Millar, was powering between Melchester's two central defenders, Lofty Peak and Dan Paconowski. Suddenly, Millar was in.

He needed one touch to control the bounce.

Then one shot.

Goal.

Melchester Rovers 0-1 Holverton Wanderers.

The goal was met with a stunned silence inside Mel Park. Now Melchester needed *two* goals against League Two's meanest defence.

Roy caught the ball that Gordon Stewart had angrily hoofed out of his net, then tossed it to Blackie Gray for kick-off. They looked into each other's eyes.

'Right then,' Roy said. 'We score two.'

'Yeah,' Blackie agreed.

But by half time – and with no more goals – Roy and his teammates trooped off. Losing. They had just forty-five minutes to win the game, salvage their season, and save their club.

'IN AN HOUR'S time we'll be in one of two places,' Kevin "Mighty" Mouse, the Melchester Rovers manager, began.

Sixteen footballers – all under the age of eighteen – sat on the rickety wooden benches that lined the walls of the Rovers dressing room, leaning forward, eyes on the boss. Melchester Rovers was a club in crisis. The older professionals had been released earlier in the season. All of them. The youth team had become the first team overnight.

And Kevin Mouse had to find a way of

motivating them. Along with first team coach, Johnny Dexter, who stood alongside him. Frankie Pepper – the club physio – was working on Blackie Gray's ankle.

'We could be sat here in one hour, defeated.' Mouse paused, the silence in the room broken by laughing coming from the Holverton dressing room on the other side of the corridor.

'Who wants that?' Mouse asked.

Roy shook his head along with several of his teammates.

'None of you?'

'No, gaffer,' Vic Guthrie, the Melchester Rovers captain, offered.

'No,' Mouse shook his head. 'Nor me. The laughing from across the corridor will be louder and we'll be able to hear it all the more because our magnificent, loyal, and long-suffering fans will be half way home and looking forward to a miserable night because we will have broken their hearts.'

More silence.

'That's one scenario,' Mouse said. 'What's the other?'

Vic Guthrie stood up. Roy felt a shiver run up the back of his neck.

'A ground full of fans,' Vic said. 'And us doing a lap of honour, gaffer.'

Lofty Peak stood up. Then Blackie. Roy too. Soon the whole team was on its feet.

'And how are we going to make that happen?' Mouse asked.

Vic cast his eyes around his team; Roy saw an unmistakable fire in his captain's eyes.

'By scoring two,' Roy said.

Mighty Mouse nodded. 'That's right, boys,' he said, raising his voice now, talking faster. 'Who has family or friends in the stands today? People who've come here to support the team, to support you?'

Every player nodded.

'You're about to run out onto the pitch,' Mouse said, eyeing each of them. 'And, when you do, I want you to look for them. Your friends, your family, all those people you know. Make them a promise: that you are going to do everything humanly possible to win this game, so that when they – and we – leave this stadium tonight, *we* leave laughing, *we* leave smiling. Understood?'

THE MELCHESTER ROVERS team sprinted onto the pitch for the second half. Roy did what he always did before kick-off and looked his teammates in the eyes. He saw belief. He saw a group of players that had the desire to turn a game, a season, a club's fortunes around.

16

Roy looked back towards the home bench. At Mighty Mouse and his first team coach, Johnny Dexter.

'We've got this,' he heard Mouse say to Dexter.

THE BEGINNING OF the second half saw Holverton hogging possession. Roy and his teammates did their best to win the ball, but it was hard. Their opponents had more experience and were bigger men. Rovers were 1-0 down. Holverton in control. And time was running out.

Forty minutes left.

Thirty.

Then twenty.

Where did time go when you were losing and needed a goal? Two goals?

After seventy minutes of giving it

everything, Roy was exhausted. And he could see the rest of the Melchester team were too. Heads down. Some crouching on the pitch, breathing hard. When Asif Mirza went down with cramp, Roy and Vic stood together and looked over at Mighty Mouse. Their manager was making gestures that they should push upfield, take risks now.

Vic put his thumb up.

Then Roy saw that, for Johnny Dexter, sitting on the bench was too much. He watched their coach stand tall and prowl the touchline, locking eyes with the fans, who seemed as dejected as the players on the pitch. Their chanting had died down. The atmosphere had drained out of Mel Park now, leaving nothing but anxiety.

Johnny Dexter gestured at the fans with both his hands, using his giant arms and huge chest to grab their attention.

'COME ON!' Coach shouted. 'Get behind the boys. We need you.'

Roy smiled at Vic as they watched Coach jog on and do the same fifty metres on.

'It's working,' Roy said as more and more of the Melchester faithful were geed up by Johnny Dexter's touchline raging.

Because now there was an atmosphere. Now there was electricity.

Johnny Dexter applauded the fans as the game kicked off again, Asif Mira receiving treatment on the pitch side.

Roy tracked the ball and watched Vic Guthrie challenge hard for – and win – it just inside the Holverton half. Now Vic looked taller, stronger. He had twenty thousand Melchester Rovers fans with him. They all did. And it helped: the noise. Inside Roy felt the energy of their chanting ripple through him.

It was time to turn the game around.

Two minutes later, Vic won the ball again and played a crisp pass to Paco Diaz, who controlled it, looked for runners ahead of him, and, spotting the goalie off his line, chipped it from thirty-five yards.

Roy ran hard – all energy now – angling into the penalty area, pushing his body to

the limit as the ball arced over the keeper's despairing dive and – smack – came down off the woodwork.

Roy Race – stumbling, scrambling, using the momentum of his run to stoop – headed the ball.

It bounced into the net.

GOAL!

Melchester Rovers 1-1 Holverton Wanderers.

Johnny Dexter was on his feet. 'Five minutes,' he shouted, deep and loud above the ear-splitting noise coming from the stands. 'Come on lads. Five minutes. One goal.'

Roy jogged back for the restart. His legs were like jelly now, like lead. Like jelly made out of lead. He had nothing left. He was not match-fit after a month out with injury.

He looked into the stand as he took deep

breaths. He heard Johnny Dexter's shouts, and saw his sister and his friend, Ffion, among thousands of others cheering them on, grabbing their Melchester Rovers shirts by the badge, willing the team on to score one more.

And Roy remembered Mighty Mouse's words in the dressing room, remembered that Rovers needed to send the fans home happy.

That's where he found the energy to do what he did next.

Melchester Rovers were passing the ball hard and fast. Stewart to Paconowski. Paconowski to Guthrie. Guthrie to Gray. Gray to Diaz. Diaz to Vernon Elliott, who turned his man, finding the space to curl a cross beyond both Holverton central defenders. To Blackie Gray.

Blackie with final ball.

To Roy. Who was onto it fast, hitting it hard, a left foot volley.

A rocket.

GOAL!

The noise made Roy's ears ring. He felt the weight of his teammates leaping on top of him, dragging him down. From under the bundled mass of his celebrating team mates, he caught sight of the scoreboard.

Melchester Rovers 2-1 Holverton Wanderers.

They'd done it.

When the roar died down, Roy jogged back to the half way line, his friend Blackie Gray beside him.

'Hold on and we're in the play-offs,' Blackie said, his voice breaking with emotion.

Roy nodded.

'The dream,' he said to his friend.

'The dream,' Blackie echoed.

AFTER TEN MINUTES of fist bumps and high fives in the heat of the dressing room, the Melchester Rovers players staggered to their seats. They were shattered. Suddenly the room was quiet. But there was no noise coming from the away dressing room across the corridor. No laughter.

Roy smiled at that and slumped onto the bench, leaning against the back of the dressing room wall. He gazed at the piles of clothes and kitbags scattered over the floor, and smelled the sharp stink of sweat coming off his teammates. Roy breathed out, stretched his leg and rotated his injured ankle. It felt okay. A little stiff, but no pain.

In the doorway stood Kevin Mouse and Johnny Dexter. Roy stared at them. He could see that they were pleased to have won, but he knew they'd already be anxious about the play-offs. The bottom line had not changed in victory today: lose the next game and it could be the end of Melchester Rovers.

Mouse coughed loudly and surveyed his squad of teenagers: the youngest professional football team in Europe.

The dressing room fell silent.

'Outstanding, lads,' Mouse said quietly. One by one, the Melchester Rovers team manager looked each of his players in the eye. 'Six months ago we were at the bottom of League Two: now we're in the play-offs, with a shout at promotion. That's down to you and what you just did out there.'

'We're going up, lads!' Vic Guthrie offered.

'Yes, Vic. The National Stadium. Promotion. League One next season,' Mouse said, then lowered his voice to a deeper tone. 'But we are not there yet. We have not done enough yet. There are three games left. We have a week before the next. Relax tonight and tomorrow. I want you to rest. You must.

You deserve to. But we've a lot of hard work to do if you want to play at the National Stadium. If you want glory. And, well, if…'

'If we want the club to carry on?' Roy finished his manager's sentence.

'Yes,' was all Mouse said in reply.

Roy understood he'd spoken out of turn. 'Sorry, boss,' he said quickly.

Mouse folded his arms. 'Apology accepted. This is an intense time. And Roy's right: the club is in danger.'

'What sort of danger?' Lofty Peak asked.

Roy had noticed that all eyes were on Mouse now. Silence again. Every player in the room knew their football careers were in jeopardy. He knew too that Lofty had more reason than most to be anxious: he'd already been released by one football club this season. If it happened again he'd be devastated.

'Leave that to Mouse,' Coach said.

'But don't we have a right to know?' Lofty argued.

'No,' Dexter snapped back. 'You don't.'

They all saw the flicker of anger in Johnny Dexter's eyes. Lofty Peak recoiled, looking at his bare feet.

Then Vic Guthrie – team captain – stood up and faced his team. 'That's it, lads,' he said, trying to refocus attention on what mattered to the players: football. 'We won today. We're all happy. Enjoy that happiness. And we've got our paintballing trip tomorrow, right? Let's enjoy ourselves, like. Then we go again. That's enough for today.'

'Listen to your captain, lads,' Coach nodded. Roy could see that Johnny Dexter was pleased with Guthrie's intervention.

Mouse held his hand up. He had one more thing to say. 'Look, the club is in trouble: you all know that. But, if we carry on working as a team and working hard, we can win promotion. And, if we win promotion, you'll all have football careers to enjoy next season. That is all I can say. It's best I keep the rest to myself. Best you lot keep doing what you do best. And you did that today, lads. I'm proud of you. And I thank you on behalf of all those fans out there.'

Roy had watched everything carefully. He was pleased that Mouse, Coach and Vic had calmed the dressing room down, but, still, deep down, he had his fears about the future of the club.

After his shower, Roy gathered his boots and shin pads and slipped them into his bag, ready to head home.

He needed to get a move on. His mum was working tonight and, because Roy's dad was ill and needed round-the-clock care, Roy had to get home. Before heading off, Roy checked his phone. He had dozens of messages congratulating him for scoring both Melchester Rovers' goals. He'd not even thought about who had scored. That didn't matter. They'd won.

Roy read the last message:

HUGO: Well done to Melchester Rovers! And to you, Roy Race.

Two fine goals. Congratulations.

Roy sat down again, stunned.

Hugo was a footballer – but not just *any* footballer. He was probably going to play in the Champions League semi-final for Melchester's city rivals, Tynecaster United, in a few days. If, of course, he could get past his recent run of bad form, and rediscover the energy that had seemed to have deserted him.

It was hard for Roy to believe that the best striker in Europe and Brazilian first choice number nine was congratulating him.

ROY: Thank you. That means a lot coming from you.

HUGO: How will you celebrate?

ROY: Looking after Dad tonight. Revising for my exams in a café in town tomorrow. I have to pass these exams or Mum will kill me. Living the dream!

Roy checked his bag. He thought about his forthcoming exams. He was doing a BTEC in Sport. He'd made a deal with his mum: he could play for Melchester Rovers if he carried on doing his course. That was why he wasn't going out on the players' paintballing trip tomorrow and why he'd be sat in a café in town going over a year's worth of notes to make sure he kept his side of the bargain.

One last text from Hugo came in, just as Roy was heading home:

HUGO: Listen to your mother. In my country not everyone can afford education.

Here, for you, it is free. I admire your hard work at college even more than your work on the football pitch, my friend.

Hugo was right. Roy's mum was right. Education was good, and whether Roy made it as a footballer or not, he was determined to keep his promise to his mum. He would study hard. He would remember as much as he could. He would make her proud in his exams.

'I WANT DAD to come to the semi,' Roy said, tucking into his chicken nuggets and chips, as well as the huge pile of steamed green beans that he'd made himself as Mum did the chips. The entire Race family – Roy, his mum and dad, and his sister Rocky – were sat round the small kitchen table, eating together, like they did every evening. The back door was open, allowing the summer evening's air to drift in and the smell of steamed green beans to drift out.

Mum chewed her bottom lip. 'I know you do, Roy. But...'

'It's a semi-final,' Roy argued. 'And... and it'll be good practice for the National Stadium.'

Roy was desperate for his dad to come and see him play again. Before he was paralysed, Dad had been Melchester Rovers' number one fan. He'd gone to over a thousand games without ever missing one. Until he got a brain tumour. Until the operation went wrong.

Mum was laughing.

'We need Dad there,' Roy pleaded. 'I'll play better with Dad there. I'll score for him. I...' Roy was silenced by an unexpected wave of emotion about his dad.

'I think Dad should go,' Rocky chipped in.

Roy adjusted the angle of his chair, eyeing his sister. What was she up to now? She was never nice to Roy. He smelled a rat.

'I'll help,' Rocky went on. 'I'll come to the match with you, not my mates. And Mum can come too. It'll be a fab family day out.'

Rocky never spoke up for Roy. She usually took a perverse pleasure in frustrating her brother, doing whatever it took to wind him up.

'Dad? You want to come, right?' Roy said, sitting back.

Dad nodded. It was all he could do. His paralysis meant that he couldn't move anything on his left side. And he barely spoke now, only managing a few words a week. Roy wanted today to be one of those moments, for him to say a big loud YES; but it wasn't to be. He could see his dad struggling to find a word, then giving up, frustrated.

'Mmm,' Dad said.

'You're right about the National Stadium,' Mum said. 'If Rovers do win…'

'We will,' Roy said.

'… then it would be good,' Mum went on. 'Your dad and I haven't been to a game for a while. We need to practise.'

'I'll be your slave for the day, Dad,' Rocky added.

Roy put his dad's fork down and faced Rocky. 'Okay, Roxanne. What it is it?'

Rocky was smirking now. 'What?' she asked.

'What do you want?' Roy had noticed that Rocky had not objected to being called by her full name. She must want something really big from him.

'What do I want?' Rocky asked.

'Yes.'

'I want to help you with Dad.'

'And?'

'And nothing.'

Roy waited. He could see it in Rocky's eyes that there was more.

He heard Dad laugh. Dad knew it too. Knew that his daughter and son were performing. For him. Dad loved their arguments, so long as they stayed playful. It was one of the few things to make him smile. That and three points for his beloved Melchester Rovers.

'Rocky,' Roy leaned towards his sister. 'Tell me what you want in the next five seconds and I'll think about it. Miss the cut and I won't. Five.'

Rocky smiled.

'Four.'

Rocky coughed.

'Three. Two...'

'I need you to take me to Tynecaster on Thursday night to watch England women play Brazil women in a World Cup warm-up game. Please…'

Roy leaned back in his chair, victorious.

Rocky continued. 'Because they're playing in Melchester for the first time and it's always been my dream to see them and there's no way I could go and watch them in the World Cup finals in France this summer so this is my only chance.'

'Rocky?' said Roy.

'But Mum won't let me go unless you come with me, so please Roy, please…'

'Stop.'

Rocky stopped.

Roy was as keen as Rocky was to watch England v Brazil. It sounded brilliant. But she didn't need to know that he was going to say yes. Not yet.

'Too much revision.' He shook his head. 'Exams.'

'You need some time off. Relax. Mum says that's okay because you work hard all week.'

'I'll be tired,' Roy added. 'Got a game on Saturday. It's a long walk to the Tynecaster ground and back.'

Dad laughed again. He knew where the conversation was going.

'I'll pay for a taxi,' Rocky pleaded. 'I've got some money.'

'I'm not sure I want to spend a whole evening with just you,' Roy said, enjoying having power over his sister. 'You're annoying.'

'I'll get Ffion to come,' Rocky said.

And, for a moment, Roy was thrown.

Ffion.

Rocky's football team coach. And, to Roy, a friend from college, doing a course in physiotherapy, who had been helping Roy recover from his injury. Who also happened to be Vic Guthrie's sister.

'So you're coming now?' Rocky teased.

Now Mum was laughing too. They all were.

Roy blushed. 'I was going to take you anyway,' he said.

'Yeah, sure,' Rocky smirked. 'Do you love her?'

'No,' Roy snapped, shaking his head.

'Mum?' Rocky was laughing hard now. 'Do you think Roy is in love?'

Roy frowned. He had a fitness session with Ffion tomorrow. He just hoped Rocky wasn't winding Ffion up like she was him. Otherwise things were about to become a lot more embarrassing.

'SO HOW'S THE ankle this morning?'

It was eight o'clock in the morning, and Roy had jogged up to meet Ffion on the Moor above town for a conditioning session. Ffion didn't work for Rovers, but Roy felt like he needed her. The club's physio was called Frankie Pepper, and she was absolutely brilliant – the only problem was she'd been put on a match day-only contract by the owner of Melchester Rovers, Barry Cleaver. So Roy had jumped at the chance when Ffion offered to help him.

The morning was warm, and the sun

streamed through the trees, casting long shadows across the sweep of mowed grass and wild heathland. Good weather for a recovery session. Less chance of muscles being stiff than if it was cold weather.

'It was a bit painful overnight,' Roy said, answering Ffion's question. 'But during the game it felt fine.'

'Good,' Ffion nodded, studying his ankle. 'Get that sock off, so I can have a look.'

Roy did as he was told, rolling his sock off and presenting his foot to Ffion.

As Ffion prodded and twisted his ankle, Roy swallowed.

'Thanks,' he said.

'Thanks? What for? Pulling your foot off?'

'For helping get me fit. Those stretching exercises. Your advice about diet. It helped a lot. And I feel stronger now. I needed it. It normally takes longer to recover. And – I'll be honest – I've never had so much energy. All those general tips you've been giving me: they work. I feel great.'

'My pleasure. When you hit that winner against Holverton yesterday you made it all worth it. Anyway. We need to take it easy today. You've played your first full-intensity match after injury. You need to be intelligent about how you train for the next few days. Some jogging on soft grass now. Then we'll do the stretching. Okay?'

Roy slipped his sock and running shoe back on and followed Ffion. They ran around the perimeter of the Moor, a huge expanse of grass with trees around the edges and – beyond the trees – a steep slope down into the city.

'What did you have for breakfast?' Ffion asked as they ran.

'Scrambled egg on toast and a fruit smoothie, homemade.'

'What was in the smoothie?'

'Banana. Kiwi fruit. Orange juice. Oats. Blackberries.'

'And what bread did you have?'

'Wholemeal.'

'Good,' Ffion said. 'Very good. Protein.

Vitamins. That's good. I hope you're paying for it out of your wages? Not asking your mum and dad to buy it all?'

'I am.'

'Good. And did you get to bed early? Vic and some of the others were up playing video games all night. That won't be doing them any good.'

'Yup. Lights out at ten.'

'Good.'

Roy frowned. Vic Guthrie being Ffion's brother. That could be a problem.

'And why is that important?' Ffion asked.

For a second Roy was confused. Why was it important that Vic was her brother? What did she mean?

'Sleep?' Ffion clarified. 'Why is it important?'

'Your body works twice as hard at repairing injuries when you're asleep.'

'Good. Now, what's going on at Mel Park?'

'Eh?'

'What's going on with Mouse and Cleaver?' Ffion slowed down to face Roy. 'Vic won't tell me anything and I need to know. I've heard rumours about the club being shut down. All sorts. I've been on the supporters' forums and everyone knows something is going on. I'm a fan: I need to know.'

Roy stopped. Ffion had changed the subject so quickly that he was taken by surprise. 'You'd best ask Vic, not me. He's captain.'

Ffion put her hands on her hips and raised an eyebrow.

'Stretch,' she ordered.

Roy stretched.

'He won't tell me anything,' Ffion said

52

in a softer voice. 'I just want to know what Cleaver says to Mouse and Dexter. From a fan's point of view. Just so we know.'

Roy said nothing.

'Stretch it like this,' Ffion told Roy. 'And hold it for ten seconds. You're not trying to strengthen it. You're just keeping it supple. You'll feel tired, but, in the long run, you'll have more energy.'

Roy focused on his ankle, feeling the tendons and muscles ache slightly, but listening to Ffion and knowing that was good. It was weird. The stretches she asked him to do were exhausting, even though he was only sitting or lying down. But long term, they filled him with energy.

'Thanks,' she said. 'You've done well today. Keep sleeping and eating protein and shakes, all that good stuff. Got it?'

'Got it,' Roy said.

And he did: he understood exactly what he had to do to keep fit and strong. What he couldn't figure out was what to do about Ffion's question. Should he pass on things he heard about Melchester Rovers to Ffion so she could share it with other supporters? Or should he stay loyal to Mouse and Johnny, and say nothing?

IT WAS QUIET in the centre of town. A sleepy sunny Sunday lunchtime. The only people Roy saw were those emerging from the Catholic church on the other side of the main square.

Roy found a seat in his favourite café, laid his college work out on the small wobbly wooden table and went to the counter where a coffee machine was gurgling, to order a drink. As he was returning to his seat, he saw a man with a grey hoodie that concealed most of his face peering in through the café window.

Automatically, Roy turned his back and kept his head down.

It was funny. Even though Roy played for a League Two football team – and not in the Premier League – his life had changed since he'd become a professional footballer. He was no longer anonymous, no longer another invisible boy. People pointed at him in the street. Johnny Dexter had warned

the whole squad to be wary of journalists who might want to make up stories about Melchester Rovers. *Keep your head down and your mouth shut.* That was his advice.

Roy settled down to focus on his college work. Today he was revising nutrition: all the foods you could eat that would make your muscles, blood and brain perform better. Roy focused, taking notes to try and remember as much as he could.

But, after a quarter of an hour and having already emptied his mug, Roy sensed a change in the light, as if the sun had gone in outside. He glanced up.

The man in the hoodie was there. Standing over him. Roy slid his seat back, freeing his legs from under the table, staring hard at the man all the while.

'Roy of the Rovers,' the man smiled, pulling his hoodie off his head.

He had short dark hair. Bright eyes. But he looked tired. More tired than the last time Roy had seen him.

Hugo.

'Let me buy you another drink, my friend?' Hugo suggested. 'And some toast with jam? It's something I like about England.'

BACK WITH A drink and toast, Hugo finally sat down. 'I saw you across the square,' he explained. 'But saw, too, you are working hard. I will only stay ten minutes.'

'Stay as long as you like,' Roy said, pushing his notes aside.

'No. You must study. I will not forget your mother. But I stay a little while. The other Tynecaster players are playing golf today. One of the club's sponsors is treating them. But it's not for me. I prefer a quiet day.

And church this morning, of course.'

'You go to church?' Roy asked, surprised.

'Always,' Hugo smiled. 'Sunday. It is church before anything. Church and family. My mother. She would be very disappointed if I did not go to church.'

'Even on a match day?' Roy asked.

'Even then. I go to church early. The church is here in town. Services at 8 a.m. and 11 a.m. It is very good. And – to be honest with you, Roy – I do not want to spend a day talking to a hundred people and playing golf, being a famous footballer. I'm tired. I need rest.'

Roy nodded and glanced at his college work.

'Ah… I know… I do disturb your work. I will go…'

'No,' Roy said, studying Hugo. He wanted Hugo to stay all day: how often did you get to sit and talk to a footballing superstar? And there was something else. Hugo looked tired or lonely, even unhappy. Roy wondered if he wished he was back in Brazil having Sunday dinner with his mum. 'Please,' Roy said. 'Stay for a bit. You know you do look tired. Are you okay?'

Hugo hesitated, looking at his hands for a moment. 'It is very difficult,' he said. 'Normally I am a man with a lot of energy. But – this season – since the English winter I am weary, is that what you say? I cannot find the energy. Our Tynecaster physios and conditioning coaches cannot help me. I can feel it. This is the end of the season. If we win our semi-final against FC Goytisolo this week, then I play in the Champions League final. But I'm not at my best. I might lose my place in the team. Then where is my dream of winning a Champions League?'

Roy said what he said next without thinking. 'You should go to Ffion. She'll sort you out.'

'Ffion? Where is that?'

Roy laughed. 'No. Sorry, Ffion is my friend. She's a girl at my college. She is good at energy. Nutrition. These weird stretching exercises. She's been helping me recover from my injury. But – with all the work we've been doing – I've never had so much energy.'

Hugo looked hard at Roy. 'It's true, Roy of the Rovers. You look alive. I must ask you a favour. Please?'

'Anything,' Roy said.

'I want to meet Ffion.'

BEFORE TRAINING – MONDAY morning – the Melchester Rovers squad gathered in what the players called the classroom. A medium-sized room with a large screen at the front that could be used as a tactics board and to watch video footage of matches. Roy sat next to Blackie, telling him about running into Hugo in the café. Blackie was the only one he wanted to tell. He'd known him all his life, and Roy knew he could trust Blackie with Hugo's secret as much as he could anyone in his family.

Mighty Mouse stood at the front of the

room. Johnny Dexter sat to the side, studying the players, some of whom were slumped in their seats.

There was an unusual atmosphere among the players today, even though the team had done the impossible and qualified for the play-offs. Roy couldn't quite work out what the problem was. But he knew there was something.

Most of it seemed to be emanating from Vic Guthrie, who kept glaring at Paco Diaz. Roy wondered if the two of them had a row when they went paintballing the day after the Holverton game.

'Sit up straight,' Coach barked. 'Paconowski. Mirza. Look at you!'

The players sat up straight. Roy too, even though he'd been pretty much upright anyway.

'So,' Mouse began. 'We know who we

have in the play-off semis. It's the lovely Kingsbay. Who remembers playing them earlier this season at Mel Park?'

'Ugly football,' Vic Guthrie volunteered. 'Nasty team.'

Roy recalled the game well.

Vic had got it right with his assessment.

'They beat us 4-1,' Mouse said. 'At Mel Park. It was horrible. Men against boys. That's what the newspapers said the next day. They scared us. And they'll be keen to scare us again, beat us even before we're on the pitch.'

'They've not met me and Blackie yet,' Lofty Peak said in a deep voice. 'We weren't here then.'

'Like you're our hardmen,' Vic Guthrie snapped. 'That's a joke.'

'*None* of you are hardmen,' Coach scoffed, interrupting. 'For a start you're all boys. And hard, you are not. You can't match them for that.'

'But don't need to,' Mouse continued. 'We will play *our* way. We will play with pace and skill and guile. We will play the beautiful game. As a team.'

Roy noticed his team mates leaning forward in their seats towards their team

manager. Mouse was great at motivating the team, creating unity.

'Some of us will,' Guthrie snapped, breaking the spell.

There it was again, Roy thought. What was going on? Guthrie was in a funny mood about something. But what?

Roy glanced at Lofty. Lofty silently gestured to Diaz, then revealed a newspaper on his lap. Roy quickly read the headline, as he took a drink from his water bottle.

DIAZ TO PACO HIS BAGS?

Young Mel Park Dynamo on his
way across the city

Roy coughed, nearly choking on his water. What was this? Paco leaving?

Roy tried to catch Paco's eye. Just to read him, see if it was true. But Paco Diaz was staring hard at the screen and was not going to look any of his team mates in the eye.

'Lads. Focus.' Johnny Dexter was talking again. 'Teamwork. Remember?'

'Teamwork means working as a team,' Vic Guthrie grumbled.

'Guthrie,' Johnny snapped. 'Are you these lads' captain or not?'

'Yes, Coach.' The tone of Vic's voice had changed now.

'Well, then. Behave like one.'

All eyes were on Mighty Mouse, who waited a few seconds for Dexter's words to sink in. The excitement about reaching the play-offs was long gone.

The Melchester Rovers that trudged out onto the training pitches were far from a team united.

Not long into the warm up, outside in the pouring rain, Roy felt Vernon Elliott nudge him and point. At the far side of the training area a Rolls Royce car pulled up like a tank, its tyres ruining the grass on the edge of the pitches.

It was Barry Cleaver, Melchester Rovers' owner.

And Roy realised that there were more problems to face in the next week than being bullied by Kingsbay, or Vic and Paco falling out.

Once the players had noticed Barry Cleaver sauntering across the training pitches adjacent to Mel Park, they all stopped and watched him approach. They knew something was going to kick off – and this time it wasn't to do with footballs.

Cleaver arrived, the tails of his long black coat trailing behind him, which, to Roy, looked like some terrible bird of prey's wings. Mighty Mouse stood, hands on hips, watching the club's owner nearly slip in a patch of mud. Johnny Dexter strode over to stand behind Mouse.

'Mr Chairman,' Mighty Mouse said. Roy noticed he said this without a smile.

'Mouse. Dexter. I came to congratulate you on qualifying for the play-offs, gents,' Cleaver said. 'Please pass my congratulations to the lads,' he added, not looking at the players.

'Thank you, Mr Chairman.'

Roy stepped close to the trio of men. If something was going to be said, he wanted to hear it.

'About the play-offs...' Cleaver smirked. 'Exciting though it is, it is *also* unexpected. I'm talking finance here. And I regret I won't have the funds to pay for hotels the night before the away leg.'

'Or the final?' Dexter cut in.

'Ha! The final,' Cleaver laughed. 'No, not for that either, if you... I mean *we* make it.'

'A bus to the games, at least, Mr

Chairman?'

Barry Cleaver frowned. 'I suppose so.'

'Well that's something,' Dexter growled. 'We can hardly walk. The National Stadium is 191 miles away.'

Barry Cleaver's narrowing eyes lingered on Johnny Dexter, then he glanced at the players, who were all listening in with Roy. 'No bonuses either, lads. No cash flow. I'm really sorry. Could be you've already had your last pay cheque from me...'

Nothing from the players. Only silence.

'But Paco Diaz.' Barry Cleaver's eyes suddenly lit up. 'Which one of you is Paco?'

Roy couldn't believe what he was hearing: didn't the club's owner know who the players were?

Paco stepped forward. 'That's me, Mr Chairman.'

'You, son, are an example to us all.

Whatever you did to get Tynecaster interested in you, all the other lads should take note. I guarantee if you can get a move out of Melchester – get a bit of income coming in – then you'll get 10% of the fee from me, tax free.'

Roy watched as all the other players stared in horror at Paco.

'But...' Paco said. 'No, Mr Cle...'

The whole team missed Barry Cleaver breaking into fits of laughter as he turned and walked away.

'I have done nothing,' Paco complained, turning to his teammates. 'It is just a story in a newspaper. Nothing to do with me.'

'Hmm,' grunted Vic Guthrie, as several Rovers players turned their backs on Diaz.

AFTER TRAINING ROY walked towards the

dressing rooms with Lofty and Paco Diaz. The rest of the team had gone ahead.

'Don't let it get to you, Paco,' Roy said. 'It's all about the play-offs. Forget Vic.'

'Yeah, Paco,' said Lofty. 'You give this club one hundred per cent. None of us know where we'll be next season.'

Roy nodded. 'Take it from Lofty, Paco. Can I tell him, Lofty?'

Lofty put a thumb up.

'Lofty was on Tynecaster's books from the age of 6 to 16. Then they booted him out. No warning. It's tough being a footballer and – like Lofty says, as long as you're giving everything you've got, which you are – Vic is talking nonsense.'

'I know,' Paco said in a mournful voice. 'But it hurts, no?'

Roy and Lofty nodded silently. Diaz shook his head and walked on, leaving Roy to wonder if he should tell Ffion what he had just seen and heard. So much going on. Would it help Ffion to know? Would it help the club? He wasn't so sure...

ROY WAS THE last to leave after training. Without the other players, their banter and laughter, the dressing rooms were stark, the pale sunlight streaming through the high frosted windows failing to take the chill out of the air.

Roy stood to go, ready to head into college to find some books he needed in the library, then stopped.

Voices.

Two voices.

'We need to do something about Vic.' It was Johnny Dexter.

'And Paco?' Kevin Mouse asked.

'Right.'

'It's divisive stuff,' said Mighty Mouse. 'And we can't have it: it affects the future of this club.'

It was too late for Roy to leave the dressing room now. Mouse and Coach would not want him to have heard what he'd heard: the two of them criticising the club captain. He decided to sit it out. He put on a pair of headphones and closed his eyes, leaning against the whitewashed breezeblock wall. If they came in he could pretend he was resting his ankle and listening to very loud music.

But Roy didn't press play. He was here now: he might as well listen. They were talking about his future as well as the club's.

The two men talking were right outside the dressing room door now. They had stopped. Roy was trapped.

'Keep him as captain?' Dexter asked.

'For now,' Mouse replied to Johnny Dexter's question. 'But if he loses it again, maybe not.'

'Replace him with?'

'Peak?' Dexter suggested. 'What do you think?'

'Peak's got experience. But he's quiet. Maybe Race?'

Roy opened his eyes wide. Now he was desperate not to be discovered. Should he hide in the toilets? Why had his name come up? He wasn't captain material. Was he?

'Hmmm,' Johnny Dexter said. 'In the future. Yes. Roy Race. No question. But he's too inexperienced now, isn't he? I mean, Race has only played half a season as a pro, but Vic's captain of Wales U17s. That's got to count for something.'

'But Roy's got something too. He just needs to toughen up a bit.'

'He needs to stop pussy-footing around Vic.'

Mouse laughed. 'It needs to happen. Vic's too big for his boots. Someone needs to bite him back before next season. Maybe Roy's the boy?'

'Next season?' Coach said. Roy noticed a sadness in his voice.

'Come on, Dex. We have to believe.'

'We have to go up, mate. We have to go up. If we don't... well, the deal's done.'

Roy swallowed. Now what? What deal was he talking about? He *so* wished he'd left with the other players.

'Isn't it?' Coach asked Mouse.

'It is,' Mouse said gravely. 'The day after we are out of the play-offs, the ground passes into the hands of the developer, Mel Park is torn down, then the club moves out of Melchester and that's it. And that man Cleaver gets his money and we're all out of a job. And that's not the worst of it.'

'No.'

'The day Melchester loses the club, loses the name... all those young lads' careers and generations of fans footballing dreams are dead.'

'That, my friend,' Roy heard Johnny

Dexter's voice fade as the two men walked away from the dressing rooms, 'is why we will *not* lose.'

Roy took his headphones off and put his head in his hands. This was bad. So bad. He wondered if he should tell Ffion. Or maybe he should keep it to himself and pretend he had never heard it.

A DAY HAD gone by. The young Melchester Rovers squad were back on the training pitches, going at it hard. Johnny Dexter gathered the players to explain the focus for the morning's main drill. Mighty Mouse was beside him. Most of the squad were waiting silently, focussed on their coach. But not all of them. Roy was watching Vic and Paco closely, desperate that their squabbling wouldn't start up again. And – to their credit – so far it had not.

'Lads,' Johnny Dexter began. 'We witnessed in that video nasty yesterday how

Kingsbay slaughtered us earlier this season. And we've seen how they played against every other team. Get the ball wide quickly, then fire balls towards the penalty area at speed, using their pace and brute force to win the ball and create chances to score.'

Dexter hesitated, then continued.

'Now. They are stronger than us. We can't change that. We're going to find ourselves alongside men twice the size of us shouldering and elbowing us off the ball. So we have to be careful. One wrong move and we give away a scorable free kick. Mouse?'

Kevin Mouse stepped forward. He was holding a clipboard, pieces of paper flapping in the breeze. 'Kingsbay score from twenty nine per cent of their free kicks within twenty-five yards of goal,' he told the squad. 'That is how they got into the play-offs, full stop. Finishing third, only just missing out on automatic promotion. Aggressive attacking. Set pieces. We give away three free kicks like that? They're probably going to score at least one. So,' Mouse posed a question, 'how do we defend those diagonal balls into our half?'

'Defend deep?' Duncan MacKay, the team's right back suggested.

'Yes. Good. We will at times. But what if they catch us on the break?'

'Track back fast,' Vic said.

'Good. Then what? You're shoulder to shoulder with a man twice your side. If you foul him they've got a one-in-three chance of a goal. You can't push him off the ball: he's too big, too clever.'

Paco put his hand up.

'Paco?'

'You tackle him clean,' Paco said.

'Then he dives,' Vic scoffed, grabbing the chance to have a go at Paco.

Paco shook his head. 'You have to tackle so clean that the referee sees you take the ball. You have to tackle perfect. Then a dive is seen to be a dive and we get the free kick.'

Vic Guthrie shook his head.

But Johnny Dexter was nodding. 'Spot on, Paco. And that is what we're going to work on now. We...'

'I've never seen Paco tackle anyone at all, let alone clean,' Vic Guthrie interrupted, causing several of the team to laugh.

Roy didn't laugh. He was worried. He'd learned a word this week: divisive. That's what Vic was being. And Roy wanted to find a way of making it stop. For the good of Melchester Rovers. The play-offs were too important for the team to be divided.

*   *   *

ROY WENT WITH seven other players and Mouse to do the drill. Four defenders and four attackers. Roy looked at who was doing his drill and frowned.

Roy was with Patrick Nolan, Blackie and Paco Diaz in attack.

Facing them in defence: Lofty, Dan, Duncan and Vic Guthrie.

Gordon Stewart in goal.

Vic versus Paco: not ideal.

'Right. I'll fire the ball in,' Mouse shouted, standing next to a bag of balls. 'Defence, I want tough, but not terminal, tackling. Try and pretend you're Kingsbay. Use force. Use shoulders. But no elbows, thank you. Attackers, I want you to use force back. And I want what Paco said. What was it, lad?'

'Tackle perfect.'

Kevin Mouse nodded. 'That's what I want. Go.'

The club manager fired the first ball in.
The drill had begun. And, at first, it went
well. Blackie and Lofty grappling for the ball.
Blackie making it through to fire past Stewart
twice. Lofty performing five precision tackles
to keep him out.

Roy was working alongside Patrick Nolan,
who was coming off worse against Guthrie.
Roy had set him up with several chances to

score, but Vic had tackled him perfectly six times out of six, Patrick not even getting a clear shot at goal. Roy could see he was lacking in confidence and was trying desperately to make it easier for him, to give him confidence. But Vic had him in his pocket

'Last set,' Mouse shouted after twenty minutes. 'This is good, lads. Very good.'

Mouse fired the ball in. Roy noticed that Vic had swapped places in the line with Dan and was targeting Paco now.

The ball flew in. Roy trapped it, turned and played it square to Paco.

Diaz pushed easily ahead of Vic, twenty yards out. He drew his leg back to shoot, Gordon Stewart dashed off his line, tightening the angles, then the tackle came in. Vic, scything first through Paco's legs, then hitting the ball at full power, sending it hard towards the corner flag.

Roy sprinted over to Paco as he got to his feet, squaring up to Vic.

'You could have broken my leg,' Paco shouted.

Vic moved closer and shouted. 'I will if you go to Tynecaster.'

They were face to face now, their eyes blazing. Everyone else had stopped to watch. The inevitable. The fight that had been brewing all week. And now Roy had to find a way to diffuse it.

ROY PUT HIMSELF between Paco and Vic. He'd decided that – in order to stop this fight shattering their dreams of promotion – he had to do something he'd never done before. He remembered what Mighty Mouse had said the day before about someone needing to stand up to Vic. So… was this the time?

No. It was not. Roy had another idea.

'Paco,' Roy said, looking into Diaz's dark brown eyes. 'I've got a problem. '

'Me too,' Paco said. 'With Vic.'

Roy shook his head. 'No, mate. I've got a problem with you.'

Roy noticed Vic's taut jaw relax just slightly as he pushed the two combatants apart with a hand on each chest. Both players stepped back, surprised that Roy was taking Vic's side.

Paco stared in horror at Roy. 'With me?' his voice came out high pitched. 'You have a problem with me? No, my friend, you have a problem with Vic. Always, for you, a problem with Vic.'

'Not this time, Paco,' Roy said. 'This time it's you.'

Vic was laughing now. Roy was aware that the other players were watching with grim fascination. And that Coach was looking on too, hands behind his back, head cocked slightly to one side, frowning.

Roy had to be careful. Very careful.

'What have I done?' Paco sounded genuinely upset. 'What could I have done to upset you, Roy?'

'You're a threat to promotion.'

'What?'

'You're a threat. Because of all the Tynecaster stuff. It doesn't feel like we're one anymore. And we need to be. Are you one of us?'

Paco stepped forward now and stared into Roy's eyes. 'Of course! I am one hundred percent Melchester Rovers. I told you that already.'

Roy heard Vic tut, like he didn't believe Paco. But Roy took Paco's hand and shook it. 'I know that. I've always known it. We all just needed to hear it. Vic needed to hear it.'

'I am Melchester Rovers,' Paco reiterated.

Roy saw some of his teammates nodding.

Now Roy turned to Vic. 'Can you see that we need you more than ever now, Guthrie?'

'Meaning?' Vic snapped.

'We need a leader, Vic. I'm not a leader.

Paco's not a leader. We need you. Without you we might as well forget about the National Stadium and promotion. None of us are going up – or saving this club – without Vic Guthrie.'

Vic was speechless for a second.

Then he seemed to change, suddenly. He took Paco's hand and shook it and moved on to the rest of the team, slapping backs, putting himself right in their faces. And, as he did, Roy could feel the tension of the last couple of days lift.

As Vic worked his captain magic among the squad, Roy glanced over to where Coach had been standing. Johnny Dexter still had his hands behind his back. He still had his head on one side. But he was no longer frowning. He was looking at Roy, nodding.

Roy smiled back. This football club. It was like being on a rollercoaster. It made him think of Ffion again, and how she wanted to find out what was going on behind the scenes at Melchester Rovers so that she could use the information to save the club.

Roy wanted nothing more in the world than to save Rovers. But he wasn't sure he was going to do what Ffion wanted. Roy was part of a team. This team. If he was going to save Melchester Rovers he was going to do it with *this* group of players – on the pitch. Wasn't that the right thing to do?

Now all he had to worry about was telling Ffion. And soon – as he'd arranged to meet her after training to take care of something first...

ROY WAS NERVOUS. And not because he was stood shoulder to shoulder with Ffion in a lift. No – he was nervous because they were on their way to the apartment of Brazilian superstar, Hugo.

'What do you think his place is like?' Ffion asked.

Roy shrugged. 'Big. Fancy. Footballery.'

'Gold furniture and a butler?' Ffion imagined. 'And... and massive windows with a view across the city? But I bet it's tasteful. I mean, you know him and like him, don't you? So it's going to be nice?'

'I dunno,' Roy said. 'I don't really know him that well, anyway. We've only met a couple of times.'

The lift stopped. The doors slid open. And there was Hugo, wearing a simple grey tracksuit. No brand. The Tynecaster centre forward grinned, introduced himself to Ffion and ushered the pair into a plush-carpeted hallway that led to the footballer's apartment.

Once inside, Roy couldn't believe what he was looking at. There was a main room with a sofa and small TV, a small kitchen area at the far side. Then two open doors. One leading to a bedroom, the other to a bathroom. Hugo's apartment was smaller than his house. It was smaller than any of his mates' houses. And there was no gold furniture. Just simple ordinary wooden chairs and a table.

This was not what Roy had expected.

On the wall by the entrance there was a photograph of a village with twenty – maybe thirty – children standing outside a low building. The children were holding up a sign saying: 'Thank you, Hugo.'

Roy stopped to study it.

'It's a school I sponsor back at home,' Hugo explained, standing next to him.

'You sponsor it?'

'I send money. To my town. It's a small town, called Amado. I know you will understand. Most of the children there are the children of my friends from the town. We never had a school like that, so... you know... now we do. My town and its people gave me everything: now I try to give them something back.'

Ffion was looking over their shoulders. 'So *you* pay for the school?'

Hugo nodded. He looked embarrassed now. 'But please. I can trust you, yes? Please don't tell anyone. It is better it is not known. It will turn the school into a circus.'

Hugo swiftly changed the subject.

'So – Ffion – Roy tells me you work with him on recovery. To find his energy. Please... I need some energy. Can you help me?'

For the next few minutes Ffion led them through a series of stretches. Arching their backs, forming a bridge with their bodies, stretching their arms and legs and stomachs, but slowly, without any intensity.

For the most time they did it in silence, Ffion's voice calmly suggesting what they do next.

Half way through their workout, Roy's phone rang. He checked the screen. His mum was calling.

'Excuse me,' he said, walking into the entrance area to speak to her, as he looked again at the photograph of the school children back in Brazil.

'Mum?'

'Roy. I need you home soon. I've got an extra shift. Can you be back by two? Look after your dad?'

'Sure.'

'And go via the market. Get some potatoes and spinach. And some meat. Your dad's iron levels are down.'

'Okay, Mum. Home in an hour.'

Back in Hugo's sitting room Ffion and Hugo were laughing, as Hugo tried to stretch his body into an inverted V shape.

'It's hard, but it's good,' Hugo gasped. 'I feel tired. But also maybe more energy. Inside. I hope Roy was right.'

'Just keep doing what I've said every other day. And sleep a fixed eight hours. Don't go to bed late. Don't lie in. But you know all this. You must have a team of physios at Tynecaster?'

'We do,' Hugo admitted. 'But it is very traditional – is that the right word in English? This is a little more like yoga, maybe?'

Ffion nodded. 'A little,' she shot Roy a smile.

'So, thank you, Ffion. May I pay you for this time…'

Ffion shook her head. 'It's a favour,' she said. 'Any friend of Roy's is a friend of mine.'

Roy noticed Hugo smile when she said this.

They left Hugo's apartment and stood in the hallway with him until the lift came. Hugo kissed Ffion on both cheeks, then shook Roy's hand. All three departed smiling.

But, in the lift on the way down, Roy had to ask. 'What were you talking and laughing about when I was on the phone to Mum? Do you mind me asking?'

Ffion turned to face Roy. She put her hand on his shoulder. 'It was so sweet, Roy. Hugo told me about his friends back in Brazil and how he misses them, you know the ones whose children are in the photograph? And that the players at Tynecaster…. he says, well, he says none of them seem like real people to him. Like his friends at home. But he says that *you* remind him of his real friends. Isn't that sweet?'

Roy felt himself blush. He didn't know why.

Then he saw Ffion studying him.

'What?' Roy said as the lift doors opened and they walked across the foyer, out past the security woman and onto the street outside.

'You've got a bit of a bromance going on there.'

They walked through town – past Hugo's church.

'Anyway,' Ffion said, still smiling, checking her watch, 'you promised you were going to tell me some inside stuff about Melchester Rovers. About Cleaver and his plans. None of the fans really know what's going on.'

'I didn't promise,' Roy said.

Ffion stopped walking. 'What? You must know loads. Come on.'

Roy turned to her. 'It's true. I do know stuff. But I need to think about it some more. I'm sorry…'

'Oh man…' said Ffion, with an impish grin. 'I thought you were going to spill everything for a second there!'

AFTER DINNER AT home, Roy and Rocky sat at the kitchen table, sheets of paper and textbooks laid out in front of them, along with two glasses of juice provided by their mum.

Rocky sighed. For the seventh time.

Roy glared at her until she looked up.

'What?' Rocky spat.

'You keep sighing. I'm trying to revise and you keep sighing.'

'Well, you keep biting your nails – which is disgusting, by the way – but you don't catch me saying anything.'

'Except you just did.'

Rocky narrowed her eyes and scowled at her brother.

'Anyway, GCSEs are easy,' Roy added. 'I don't know why you're so wound up.'

'GCSEs are miles harder than your course. Your course is for dimwits who can't do A Levels.'

'It's vocational, actually,' Roy countered.

Rocky sniggered. 'You don't even know what vocational means, idiot. So shut up.'

'You shut up.'

'MUM!' Rocky was shouting now. 'Roy's telling me to shut up.'

Roy heard Mum's footsteps. Loud footsteps. Mum was coming to tell them off and she wanted them to know it.

'Don't you remember the deal we made with her about the game on Thursday?' Roy whispered before she reached them.

'Oh yeah,' Rocky said. 'That.'

The door opened. Mum's face was pink, her eyes large and threatening.

'What?'

Rocky attacked. 'Please let me work in my room. Roy's really annoying.'

'No.'

'Why not?'

'You never work properly when in your room. You mess about. Go on your phone. I want you to work here where I can see you. For two hours. Full stop.'

'I'm tired.'

'So am I. I've done three shifts today. The bank at five. Then the care home. Then back there again this afternoon. And for rubbish money. Why do you think I have to do that?'

'Because you didn't try at school,' Roy and Rocky said together.

'Exactly. If I could, I'd go and do a course on counselling, for instance. And I'd be good

109

at it too. I'd get a qualification and set up a business. If I had the chance of going back to school like you two. For free.'

'So do it,' Roy said.

'Ha ha.'

Roy looked his mum in the eye. 'I can help now. With the money.'

Mum shook her head. 'Maybe you can today, but there are no certainties about the future. We all know Rovers are in trouble. And there are no guarantees we'll get promoted. So we don't know if you'll have money in a couple of weeks' time. I mean… if we do go up, then…'

'…then I'd be on regular money – and better money. In League One.'

'If this… if that,' Mum said quietly. 'You can't predict the future, Roy.'

'Why don't you do a deal, then?' Rocky interrupted.

Roy glanced at his sister. What was this? One of Rocky's interventions usually meant trouble.

Mum sighed. 'What deal?'

'If Rovers get promoted,' Rocky explained. 'And if Roy gets a League One pay rise, then you go to college and he pays.'

Roy leaned forward. 'Yes. That's a good deal.'

Mum ran her hand through her hair. 'I need to check on your dad.'

'We need an answer,' Rocky pressed.

'I don't know,' Mum said. 'It's Roy's money.'

'No it's not,' Roy said, remembering what Hugo had said to him about his village back in Brazil. 'It's ours. Look, Mum. You and Dad have given me everything, now I want to give you something back.'

Roy and Rocky followed Mum into the front room.

'Mum?'

'I need to talk to your dad about it,' Mum said, holding her hand up.

Roy glanced at Dad.

Dad winked.

And Roy decided he was going to talk to Dad about it first. And not just about Mum. About everything. There was so much going on in his head. Mum. Rovers. Ffion. College. Hugo. Even if he couldn't talk back, he could listen and give him some idea what he was thinking.

16

THAT EVENING – AFTER he'd done his college work – Roy and Dad sat in the front room, curtains drawn, TV on, Roy on the floor next to his dad in his wheelchair.

FIFA time.

Roy was playing as England women's team, guiding them through the groups stages to qualify for the finals in France. In the last group game, it was England 4-2 Netherlands. Dad was watching, as usual, supporting Roy with nods with a 'mmm' for yes and an 'uh-uh' for no when Roy had choices to make about strategy and team selection.

Once Mum and Rocky had gone out to pick up something for Rocky at the local retail park, Roy paused the game and turned to his dad.

'Can I ask you about something?' Roy said.

'Mmm.' Dad nodded.

Roy wondered how to start. Then he remembered what his Dad had been like when he could talk. He'd been direct. You didn't mess about with Dad. You just went straight for the point. And Roy knew well that his dad was still like that: he might not be able to speak or move the left side of his body, but he was still the same thinking loving man. Roy just could say it.

'Mum wants to go to college,' Roy explained. 'I'm getting regular money now. I want to pay for her.'

Roy watched Dad's face. He smiled a half

smile with the right side of his face. Then a nod.

Roy took it as a good sign. He pushed on. 'But she's worried that if we don't go up I'll not have a contract.'

Dad nodded.

'But I want to do it anyway. I want to help her. And this is the one thing I can do to help

her, help all of us. It's the one thing in my control. But she wants me to wait.'

'Mmm,' Dad said.

'You think I should wait?'

'Mmm.'

'I know,' Roy frowned. 'You're right. She's right. But I just wish there was something I could do to make it happen without *having* to wait.'

Dad coughed and tried to speak, but his words failed in his throat.

Roy smiled and waited.

Dad tried again, but still the words wouldn't come.

'There's no rush, Dad,' Roy said.

Then Dad tried for a third time.

'Go up,' Dad said.

Roy stared at his Dad. The words hit Roy like a tackle from behind.

Go up.

Two short words.

Two short words that Roy was now even more determined to make happen.

So that was it. Melchester Rovers had to win promotion. Not just so Roy and his dad's club didn't die. Not for Roy's career as a professional footballer. But because it meant his mum could go to college. It meant he could improve his family's life. It meant *everything*.

And Roy knew would use every atom in his body to make it happen.

But he wanted to ask Dad one more thing.

'Dad?'

'Mmm.'

'There's something else.'

'Mmm.'

Dad looked tired now. Roy didn't want to wear him out, but, well... he needed his dad.

'Ffion is asking me to find out what's going on at Mel Park,' Roy explained. 'You know… all the things I've told you about Mr Cleaver and Mighty Mouse.'

'Mmm,' Dad said, which confused Roy. Was he saying he should share the club's secrets with Ffion?

'I think she wants to know things she can share online to try and stop Mr Cleaver hurting the club.'

'Mmm.'

Roy could see Dad was becoming more agitated. He realised he had to ask a clear question.

'Dad.'

'Mmm.'

'Do you think I should tell Ffion what I hear Mighty Mouse and Johnny Dexter talking about?'

'Uh-uh.' Dad said, shaking his head vigorously.

That was a very clear answer. No.

Dad was right. Roy realised he was going to have to disappoint Ffion – and he did not want to do that at all.

'RIGHT LADS. EIGHT-A-SIDE. Forty-five minutes.'

They'd warmed up. They'd stretched. They'd done a couple of basic drills. Now Johnny Dexter had the Melchester Rovers squad sitting in a circle on the short cropped grass of the training pitch. The pitch was hard, the soil dry. It was a warm May morning. A bee weaved its way between two of the team – Lofty Peak and Satioshi Nagamatu, the club's mercurial midfielder – who were sitting together on the grass with Vernon Elliott.

Summer.

The football season was over.

Unless you were one of the teams involved in the play-offs.

Two women in high-vis jackets wandered across the training pitches. One of them had a camera on top of a spike, and the other, a hundred yards away, took readings on some sort of device.

'Surveyors,' Roy heard Satioshi say. 'My mum is an architect. I've seen them doing this before. They're measuring up, getting ready to build something.'

A rumble of discontent passed through the squad. Roy reflected that there was something missing from the team, even though they were close to pulling off the seemingly impossible and getting Rovers to the play-off final.

'This,' said Johnny Dexter, 'is the last full training session before the first leg of the play-off semi-final. So I need you to ignore those two ladies, who are only doing their jobs, and concentrate. We need to *focus*, lads.' He paused. 'Now, we're at home first, so we need to win. A draw would be disappointing. A defeat, catastrophic. And you know that the more effort you put into this training session the more chance we have of getting the win we need. Got it?'

The circle of young footballers shouted 'Got it' back at their coach. Some of them were on their feet, ready to play.

'One more thing,' Johnny stopped them. 'Sit!'

The players sat.

'I want you to look at each other.'

The players looked confused.

'Go on,' Johnny insisted. 'Look at each other.'

The players glanced at each other, smirking. Some making gestures.

Coach shook his head. 'There are sixteen of you. Sixteen individuals. Right?'

'Right, Coach,' some of the players chorused.

'You've each contributed to getting us into sixth place in League Two and the play-offs. Every one of you. But there's something even more important than each of you. Can anyone tell me what it is?'

'You, Coach,' Blackie Gray called out to laughs from around the circle.

'Yes. Me. Of course, me.' Johnny Dexter was grinning. 'No, something else. Something even more significant – believe it or not – than me.'

'The team,' Roy called out.

'No. Something closer to each of you,' Coach said.

Roy felt a warm breeze waft across the playing fields. He lifted his water bottle to his lips and wondered what Johnny was going on about.

'What I'm talking about is relationships,' Coach explained. 'Is that each of you on the pitch at any one time has ten footballing relationships with the others. Right?'

'Right, Coach.'

'That's what makes a team. If you let one of those relationships weaken, then we're all weaker. So...' Johnny Dexter looked at Roy. 'Roy and Vic. Off the pitch, you don't get on, right?'

'Right,' called out Vic, before Roy could even process the question.

'And Vernon. You've had some trouble with Patrick this week, right? And Lofty, you with Paco, right?'

Patrick and Vernon smiled at each other.

Johnny Dexter surveyed his team of young players. 'I want you to think about your relationships in this group. I want you to make sure they're all as good as they can be. I want Vic to have Roy's back more than any other player in the team. I want Lofty to fill the gap when Paco surges forward. The more you struggle with each other off the field, the more I want to see you being there for each other on it. Then... and *only* then can we win this match. Then – *only* then – will we get to the National Stadium. Am I understood?'

Out of the corner of his eye Roy saw Lofty lean over to Paco and shake his hand. He smiled. Then Vic walked over to him. Roy stood up to meet him, and Vic clasped his hand. Hard.

'On the pitch, Roy, I've got your back like no other,' Vic said, eyes burning into Roy's.

'Right back at you, Vic,' Roy said, staring back.

There was a long silence as the rest of the players waited to see what would happen next.

'Off it,' Vic grinned, glancing at his audience. 'So long as I don't hear a bad word about you from our lass, then we might be okay...'

'Noted,' Roy said.

'Now,' Coach said. 'This training session will set the tone for our play-off campaign. I want one hundred per cent.'

Roy shuddered deep inside. This was it.

He was going to give it everything.

THEY PLAYED HARD. Sixteen players trying to win, control and use the ball on half a football pitch. Shoulder barges. Strong tackles. Aerial challenges.

Roy did what Johnny had asked. He

waited for tackles to come in, then gave it everything back, using his body weight to counter shoulder charges, skipping over heavy tackles, backing into his opponents.

Vic was on the other team, constantly hacking at Roy's feet, pushing and shoving, trying to knock Roy off his stride, testing his fear of being tackled and badly injured. But never fouling. They went at it full on, the

two of them. It was a personal battle. Vernon and Patrick were doing the same, one to one. Pairs of players pushing each other to the limit, creating an intensity Roy hadn't felt in training before.

'It's going to be the hardest game of your lives, lads,' Coach shouted fifteen minutes in. 'Do you think the Kingsbay players are telling themselves that they are the team we are going to roll over, like this story is all about us?'

Roy stopped and looked at Coach.

Several other players did the same.

Coach shook his head. 'No. They'll be telling each other that *we* are the ones *they* are going to roll over. Their story is Kingsbay going to the National Stadium after battering us for the third and fourth times this season. They think *we're* a footnote in *their* story. Is that going to happen?'

Sixteen voices shouted back.

'No!'

'That's right,' Coach grinned. 'Now. Harder. I want fifteen more minutes of this. The harder you work now, the better chance we have of a result on game day. Got it?'

Vic upped his intensity. Roy ended up on the floor several times, but he didn't wince, didn't complain.

After one particularly forceful shove, Vic put his hand out to lift Roy back to his feet.

'I need you to know that I'm doing this for you, Race,' he said, his face serious. 'I figure that the more times I put you on the floor, the better chance we have of getting to the National Stadium, based on what Coach has said.'

Roy brushed himself down. 'What can I say, Vic? Just a big thank you from me. Thank you so much for being so brutal.'

Roy thought he caught Vic smiling. But it was a fleeting moment.

By the end of the training session, Roy had worked out why Coach had pitted him against Vic, Vernon against Patrick. The team was more together than ever now. Johnny Dexter was a genius.

THERE WAS SOMETHING different about the team after the training session. That missing ingredient that Roy had been thinking about. Something you couldn't quite name or describe.

A buzz?

An electricity?

Roy never could find the right word for it. But it was there. Melchester Rovers FC were there. He studied his teammates and saw something in them all.

'Excellent, lads,' Coach said. 'Excellent work. Play with that attitude and – with

133

luck on our side – we'll take Kingsbay down on Saturday.'

Roy grabbed the ball bag from the side of the pitch and gathered the three balls they'd been using during the practice game. It was something he'd always done. He remembered really early on – when he was playing for Grimroyd under-sevens or under-nines – that his dad had said he should help tidy up, make sure the coaches weren't left to clear up after the kids. Roy didn't hear much from his dad now. But anything he could remember that his dad had told him over the years, he made a point of doing.

Roy jogged to catch up as his teammates walked back to the dressing rooms. Johnny Dexter was at the rear.

'I overheard you earlier in the week,' Johnny said quietly, as they walked side by side.

For a moment Roy's heart jumped in his chest and he wondered if Johnny was talking about Roy and Ffion, about spying on him and Mighty Mouse.

'Coach?'

'Sorting Diaz and Guthrie out,' Coach said. 'Clever psychology. I was impressed. The way you helped them question their game by making them feel good about themselves. You did a lot to help calm everyone down.'

'Thanks, Coach.'

'You've got a good head on your shoulders for a kid. You're loyal. Mouse and I, we like that. We're pleased with you. We trust you.'

Roy dropped the bag of balls outside Coach's office and went to join the rest of his teammates in the showers. His mind was a jumble of thoughts. Pleased to be praised by Coach. Terrified that he'd been considering doing the exact opposite of what Coach was praising him for: being loyal.

But amid all that conflict and his swirling thoughts, Roy had one constant. He was going to prove his loyalty by giving everything he had to Melchester Rovers, and to his family.

All he had to do now was win a play-off semi-final, and do his best in the exam that he'd been revising for all month.

'LAST ONE,' ROCKY grinned.

'Okay.'

Roy and Rocky were revising. Roy, physiology. Rocky, English Lit. They'd been helping each other for two hours.

'Question twenty,' Rocky said. 'Why do your muscles burn when you're doing intense exercise?'

Roy breathed in. 'Right,' he said. 'They burn because when the muscles produce energy from glycogen and there's not enough oxygen, then the body produces lactic acid. And that makes a burning sensation.'

Rocky nodded. 'Good boy, Roy. Bang on.'

'So how many did I get?' Roy asked.

'Out of twenty?' Rocky smirked, pouring orange juice out of a carton into her glass.

Roy felt uneasy now. His sister was trying to wind him up. He needed at least fifteen to feel confident about his exam tomorrow. He noticed that Mum was in the doorway now: she wanted to know his result on the practice test paper. Mum had stayed out of the way, trying not to put pressure on Roy; but he knew she was listening, making sure he was working hard. Dad was in the front room watching the Champions League semi-final. Tynecaster versus FC Goytisolo of Spain. The game was already into the second half.

'You scored,' Rocky said, drumming on the table, '...a fantastic SIXTEEN out of twenty.'

Roy punched the air. That was good.

Good for him.

'...which means, Roy Race, you are not quite as stupid as we all thought you were.'

'Well done, Roy,' Mum said, putting her hand on Roy's shoulder. 'Now you need to stop. Relax. Go and watch the football. You've both been revising for hours and you need rest as well as hard work.'

'I'm off to bed,' Rocky said. 'What time are we off to the match tomorrow, Roy?'

'Kick-off's at eight. So, we could head off about half-six?'

'Great,' Rocky said. 'Thanks.'

'Come here,' Mum said, giving her two children a big hug, so they all ended up in one great scrum in the middle of the room.

'Muu-um!' Rocky complained.

'Oh let me,' Mum said. 'It's just so good to see you two getting on so well. It's lovely.'

'Hmm,' Rocky said.

'It's just a truce, Mum,' Roy added. 'After I've taken her to England versus Brazil tomorrow, all-out war will resume.'

'If not before...' Rocky laughed.

Roy stood up, grabbed his juice and a couple of bananas, and went to join his dad in the front room.

'What's the score, Dad?'

Dad put two fingers up.

Roy laughed. His dad might not be able to speak, but he still had a sense of humour.

'How's Hugo doing?'

Dad stuck his thumb up now.

And Roy glanced at the screen to see his new friend take the ball on the edge of the penalty area, half turn then spray a twenty yard pass to the left. Then he turned and powered towards the FC Goytisolo goal.

Roy leaned forward. He felt torn. On the one hand he didn't want to see Tynecaster win the Champions League semi-final. On the other, he was thrilled to see his friend playing with such verve.

It was too soon to say whether Ffion was helping Hugo with his game. But, the way he was playing, he certainly looked sharp.

Roy settled down with his dad to enjoy the match. This was good. Mum was right. He needed to take his mind off his exam – and everything else that had been piling up on him over the last few days.

Roy stumbled out of the shaded air-conditioned chill of the college exam hall into the bright afternoon light outside college. It was warm. A breeze drifted through the trees surrounding the concrete stairway up to college. He blinked, rubbed his eyes, shuddered at the noise of the traffic. It had been so quiet in the exam hall.

How had he done in the exam? That was all he could think about.

Roy wasn't sure. But he knew he'd done his best. He'd revised. He'd concentrated. All the things you're supposed to do. Now he just wanted to go home and chill before the England-Brazil match at Tynecaster tonight.

Then he saw Ffion, hands in her pockets, leaning against a wall. Waiting for him. He felt his heart-rate pick up.

'How was it?' Ffion asked.

'Good,' he said. 'I think I did okay.'

Ffion put her arm around Roy and squeezed his shoulder. 'Well done. It can't be

easy. What with the football and home and stuff. You live an intense life, my friend.'

They sat down on the row of benches by the bus stop. Three lads were throwing a small rucksack around. A car went past and Roy heard a child's voice call out his name. There was a dog barking in the distance.

'But enough about you,' Ffion asked, rubbing her hands together. 'What's going on at Mel Park? Any intel for me?'

Roy shook his head.

'Nothing?' Ffion pressed.

This was it, then, Roy realised. This was where he was going to be frank with Ffion. He'd listened to his dad and overheard Mouse and Coach and made up his mind. Saying no to Ffion was something he desperately didn't want to do, but had to do. Better to be honest than lie. His dad had always told him that.

'Look,' Roy said, lowering his voice, 'I wish I could tell you everything. I know stuff. I see stuff. I'm not going to pretend I don't. But it doesn't feel right saying what's supposed to be private to the club.'

'But I'm a fan... we're more important than the players... the manager... We... ' Ffion stopped herself and stayed quiet for a few seconds. 'Fine,' she said. 'That's fine. I understand.'

'I'm sorry.'

'Don't be.'

Roy felt guilty now. Like he was disappointing Ffion. The last thing he wanted to do in the world. He wanted her to like him, more than anything.

'I'd tell you if I could.'

Ffion put her hand up. 'Shut up, Roy. I told you. I get it. It's fine. Subject closed. I'm happy.'

She did not look happy.

As they'd been sitting there at the bus stop, the sun had gone in. The breeze felt chilly now.

'I wanted to ask you something,' Roy said, eager to break the uneasy silence.

Ffion turned to face him. She pushed a strand of red hair behind her ear.

'What's that?'

'I'm going to the England match at Tynecaster tonight,' Roy told her. 'Versus Brazil. I'm taking Rocky. Do you want to come?'

Ffion shook her head.

'It'll be good,' Roy said.

'I know it'll be good. But I'm going with some other people,' Ffion replied.

Roy felt a surge of disappointment and wondered who the other people were. Wondered too if he should have told her something small about what was going on with Cleaver and Mighty Mouse. Then she'd come. Then she'd like him.

'You need some quality time with Rocky. You're her big brother. She looks up to you. You taking her to this match is a big deal for her.'

Roy laughed.

'What?' Ffion looked cross.

'She doesn't look up to me at all. She thinks I'm an idiot.'

Now Ffion was shaking her head. 'You're good at reading the game on the pitch, Roy Race. Your teammates' runs, who's going to put the ball where. But off the pitch? Less so.'

'I don't...'

'Take your sister to the match. You and her. Make her feel like she's the most important person in the world. She needs it. Especially from you.' Ffion glanced up. 'Your bus,' she pointed, then jumped up. 'Enjoy the game.'

Then Ffion was gone.

Roy found a seat on the bus and slumped into it. His head hurt. What was all that about? Was she cross with him? Was she right about Rocky? What was going on? Then he smiled.

What had she said?

You're good at reading the game on the pitch, your teammates' runs, who's going to put the ball where. But off the pitch? Less so.

Maybe she was right.

Roy took out his phone to text Rocky.

21

ROY AND ROCKY got to Tynecaster's stadium early and sat right next to the players' tunnel, where they could hear shouts and doors banging, laughter. As close to the action as they could get.

Tynecaster's stadium was huge. A twenty-first century amphitheatre. Roy could hear the voices of the players as they warmed up. He remembered the last time he had been here when the stadium had been full. The FA Cup tie in January. He'd scored once. Nearly twice. But Hugo had finished Rovers off, and sent them out of the Cup.

Roy breathed in and gazed at the stands. He would come back here one day and score a winner. If there were any stadium in the world where he would do that it would be this one. He swore to himself.

'You have to take photos of me when the players are behind me,' Rocky demanded, interrupting his fantasies. 'Okay?'

'Fine,' Roy said. 'But it'll be better when they come back in. You'll see their faces then.'

'Whatever, Roy. Just make sure you do it.' Rocky pulled a magazine out her bag. A copy of *She Kicks*. 'Have a look,' she said, pointing at a team picture of the England team.

'I know what the England team look like, Roxanne.'

'You know them?'

'Of course!'

'Well, make sure you get some good pictures. Okay?'

Roy nodded.

By the time the players lined up in front of the main stand for the national anthems, facing most of the fans, the bottom tiers were full all the way round. Roy estimated there were twenty thousand fans there, and he felt a shiver of excitement up his spine. This was his first England match. His first international. He looked at the players, backs straight, shoulders square. He could see they were proud.

Dreams do come true. He knew that now. Perhaps, he thought, one day, he could be out there in an England shirt too.

ENGLAND VERSUS BRAZIL was a game of two halves.

The first half was cagey, both teams sounding each other out. Then, after eighteen minutes, Brazil were given a penalty and Rocky was on her feet, raging.

'Ref!' she screamed.

But the penalty stood. The Brazilian forward stepped up to take the spot kick.

Goal.

England 0 – Brazil 1.

The second half was better. England equalised with a cracker, a well worked team goal with a beautiful finish. Then, out of nowhere, England got the winner with a screamer from outside the penalty area, at which point Rocky grabbed Roy.

'I want to go to the next game! And the one after that! Can you get season tickets to watch England? I want to go to France. To the World Cup...'

Rocky's voice tailed off, her arms still

around her brother.

AFTER THE GAME Rocky turned to face Roy.
The England players were coming off.

'Now!' she said. 'Take some pictures!'

Roy took a stream of photos, trying to get
Rocky in the shot and each of the England

players as they were applauded off the pitch.

And then there was someone waving at him. A man. Dark hair. Wearing a suit.

'Roy?' he shouted. 'Roy of the Rovers? Come down. Meet some players.'

Hugo.

Roy felt the eyes of everyone around the players tunnel on him as he and Rocky walked to the bottom of the stand and Hugo let them through a low gate.

Rocky looked nervous.

'Come down,' Roy said, remembering what Ffion had said about making her feel special. 'I want Hugo to meet my sister.'

Hugo shook Roy's hand, then Rocky's.

'This is Rocky. My sister,' Roy said.

Hugo bowed. 'My pleasure,' she said. 'Any sister of Roy Race is my sister, too. I owe your brother a lot.'

Rocky said nothing. She looked paralysed

as they stood in the tunnel, the lights from a TV crew shining in the faces of a trio of Brazil players.

'So you like to watch England play?' Hugo asked Rocky.

'It's my first time,' Rocky stuttered.

'How do you like it?' Roy noticed that Hugo was speaking gently, trying to put his sister at ease.

'I love it,' Rocky beamed, beginning to relax.

'Will you go to the World Cup, maybe?' Hugo asked. 'This summer? In France?'

Rocky's face lit up. 'I would love to,' she said. 'It would be a dream. But... it's expensive. But next time? Definitely.'

'Yes,' Hugo frowned. 'But the next World Cup? It is in New Zealand. Very much more expensive.'

Rocky shook her head. 'No. You don't

understand. You see, I'll be playing in that one. For England.'

Hugo nodded. 'Okay. I will see you and Roy there.' Then he leaned out between Roy and Rocky to fist-bump the last of Brazil players walking past. When they'd all gone by his face looked different, a slight frown, but his eyes lit up.

'I say to you that I owe you a favour. For helping me. I am new player thanks to you and Ffion.'

Roy shrugged. 'It's Ffion,' he said. 'Not me. You don't owe me anything.'

Hugo shook his head. 'I owe you very much. Your friendship has helped me. Also Ffion's advice.'

'Well...' Roy felt himself blushing. He heard an echo of Ffion's voice saying *Bromance*.

'So,' Hugo faced Rocky. 'I want to thank

your brother. He is too humble. But I know he loves his sister. So… my thank you gift to your brother is for you both – and Ffion – to go to France to watch the World Cup this summer. I will pay for hotel, travel, tickets, food. How is that?'

'No,' Roy shook his head. 'It's too much.'

Rocky shoved Roy. 'He means yes, Mr Hugo. He's not as good at speaking English as you are. He gets confused.'

Hugo laughed again.

'Talk to your mother and father,' Hugo said to Rocky. 'As I have said, I owe your brother a big debt. This is my way of trying to do the right thing.'

Somebody from behind a TV camera called Hugo's name.

'I must go,' said Hugo. 'I am ambassador for Brazil football. I must go on television.'

And, with that, he was gone. Roy watched

him disappear down the tunnel.

Roy felt his sister's gaze on him. He turned to her.

'Please?' she said. 'Please take me to the World Cup.'

'Let's ask Mum,' Roy said. 'But I'll do my best, Rocky. Promise.'

Friday morning. The Melchester team gathered on the training ground as usual. Johnny Dexter was talking to Vic Guthrie. Roy had already noticed that Johnny was not in his training gear. He also noticed more surveyors, three women and one man with clipboards, all wearing hard hats, measuring up the grounds around Mel Park.

'Lads,' Coach shouted. 'Gather round.'

The players formed their usual semi-circle. Vic Guthrie stayed at the front with Coach.

'I'm leaving you in your captain's hands today, lads,' Coach said. 'Once he's finished with you I want you to go and eat together in the canteen. Then get home. Relax. Get a good night's sleep, and I'll see you all back here at midday tomorrow. Three o'clock kick-off. Happy?'

Several players nodded, called out, 'Yes, Coach.'

'Good. Right. Vic. Over to you.'

Vic Guthrie faced his teammates and looked each of them in the eye, not speaking for a few seconds.

'As you know,' Vic began. 'I was born to captain the Wales rugby team. But... well, that didn't work out. So I have to captain you lot instead.'

'You're too small, butty,' Gordon Stewart called out in a mock Welsh accent.

'Maybe,' Vic said, not to be distracted. 'But that childhood fantasy we all have. You know the one? The sporting pinnacle you'd like to reach. Mine was to captain Wales. And, on the day before the biggest game in the history of Welsh rugby, I would lead a Captain's Run of my players and inspire them to a great victory. You know the sort of thing?'

Roy smiled. He remembered his dream. It wasn't hard. He was living it, right now.

'So that's what we're doing,' Vic said.

Roy studied Vic Guthrie and couldn't work out what it was. He was different today. Bigger. More of a leader, somehow.

'So, we run for half an hour,' Vic explained. 'We stretch. Then we eat. That's it. Now, follow me. This is my Captain's Run. This is my dream coming true.'

Then they were off. A steady pace round the two football pitches where they'd trained every day since August. Past the hole in the fence where Roy sneaked in and gate-crashed the Rovers youth team trials – and had first met Vic, the then captain of the youth team.

Now *they* were the first team. Now *they* were two games from the National Stadium.

As they ran, Vic gave them his best inspirational chatter.

'We've talked a lot about teamwork this week. And I've let you all down by being the weakest link in the chain when I'm supposed to be the strongest.'

Roy listened to the sound of his teammates running, the steady pounding of feet, the measured breathing. No one spoke. This was heavy stuff. Vic Guthrie didn't admit he'd got something wrong every day.

'So, Diaz. I want you lead my Captain's Run.'

'Vic?' Paco sounded confused.

'It's my way of being your leader. Asking you to lead me.'

Paco was alongside Vic now. Roy smiled.

Paco thought it was a trick, some big joke that was about to explode in his face.

'I want everyone to see that I trust you, that I've got your back. Then they'll know that if I've got your back, then I've got their too. Even… well, even Race's.'

Roy heard Gordon and Lofty and some of the others laughing.

'How about letting Roy lead your

Captain's Run, then?' Blackie Gray called from the rear.

Vic turned and shouted back. 'I'll make some sacrifices, Blackie. But not to him.'

Now everyone was laughing. Laughing and running as a tightly packed unit, Paco Diaz grinning as he led from the front.

AT THE END of the run the team lay out on the grass and stretched.

'Gently,' Vic coached, prowling around watching each of the players. 'Nice and easy. No point in ripping any muscles. You're just taking the tension out of your legs, your core, your shoulders. Don't pull too hard.'

Next they ate together. Chicken. Pasta. Glasses of water. Fruit.

Then, one by one, the players left the canteen. Vic stood at the door, giving each of them a hug.

'Tomorrow!'

'Yeah. See you then.'

The whole squad left the canteen smiling. Thanks, Roy knew, to Vic.

Roy was the last to get up. Vic stopped him in the doorway.

'What you said in training earlier this week about me being a leader?' Vic said.

'Yeah?' Roy wondered what was coming now. He could never work Vic out. Was he going to be nice Vic, or nasty Vic?

'It was a good point,' Vic conceded.

'Right.'

'So thanks.'

'You're welcome, Vic,' Roy said.

For a few seconds there was a silence between the two players.

'You can go now,' Vic said, scowling. 'Don't think I'm gonna hug you.'

Roy nodded and walked down the narrow corridor, down the stairs with photos of former Melchester Rovers players – like Johnny Dexter, Hotshot Hamish and Kevin Mouse – on the walls, hoisting endless cups and trophies above their heads. The glory days. The legacy of the once mighty Melchester Rovers.

Roy made his way outside.

Then he was alone, heading away from Mel Park. Roy didn't look back. The next time he saw the Rovers stadium in all its glory, he'd be about to play in one of the biggest games in the club's history. Bigger, even, than those European and FA Cup finals.

Those games had been about winning trophies, about glory.

Tomorrow's was about survival.

MATCH DAY. ROY woke to hear the neighbour's dog – Hammer – barking. The postwoman was on her way up the street. Roy felt calmer than he ever had.

The sun was shining directly into his room, illuminating his Melchester Rovers poster from the beginning of season 2018-19. He looked at the players. None of them were at the club anymore. Only Mouse, K. and Dexter, J. remained, two suits among the red and yellow strips.

Next year, Roy thought, *I could be on that poster.*

If there was a poster.

If there was a Melchester Rovers.

There was a knock at the front door. Roy leapt out of bed, grabbing his tracksuit off the floor. Yes, Johnny had said have a lie in. But Roy wanted Mum and Dad to have a lie in. And there was no way Rocky was going to emerge from her bedroom. Not before eleven.

He pulled on his tracksuit and scrambled – as quietly as he could – down the stairs at speed, making sure he didn't slip on the worn carpet that was coming away on the last two steps.

Roy said thank you as the postwoman handed him a parcel and a slim white envelope.

'Good luck today, Roy Race,' she said.

Roy felt a twinge in his stomach, a flutter in his chest: pre-match nerves kicking in already.

Both the parcel and the envelope were addressed to him. Roy opened the parcel carefully.

Inside there was a string of football match tickets and some other documents. A hotel voucher. Some flight tickets. Roy studied them for a few seconds. His first thought was that Melchester Rovers were going on some sort of summer tour. But no. That was not on the agenda. Then he looked more closely. At the tickets.

ENGLAND v SCOTLAND on June 9
ENGLAND v ARGENTINA on June 14
JAPAN v ENGLAND on June 19

'What…?' Roy gasped. These were from Hugo. Tickets to go and watch England in the World Cup in two weeks' time. He looked more carefully. Tickets for four people. Roy crept upstairs to knock quietly on Rocky's door, excited to tell his sister about the morning's delivery.

'Go away,' Rocky shouted.

'You'll want to see this,' Roy said.

Rocky appeared at the door. She was wearing Melchester Rovers pyjamas. Roy did his best not to laugh. Instead he handed her the tickets. Then he watched his sister

gasp, grin, then her eyes fill with tears.

'He called Mum earlier in the week,' she gasped. 'He said he'd do it: I never believed he would.'

And – as Rocky went to tell Mum the tickets had come – Roy opened the envelope. It was his exam result from earlier in the week. There were four possible results: fail, pass, merit, distinction. Roy looked further down the piece of paper and read one word:

MERIT

He smiled. Merit was good. Very good.

THE REST OF the morning was about getting Dad ready for the match. Mum had a short shift at the care home. Nine till eleven, so Roy was on duty.

The weather forecast was great. Sunny. No rain. They wouldn't need coats. Roy helped Dad in and out of the shower, then sorted his breakfast out. All the time he did this, Roy chattered to his dad about the World Cup in France, about getting Mum on a university course, about anything but the game. He couldn't think about the game.

Roy had to focus.

On getting Dad ready for the match.

That was the hard thing. Dad had not been to Mel Park for ages. What if something went wrong? What if Dad felt unwell during the game and Roy saw him from the pitch? What would he do then?

When Roy knocked a cup of tea over, he felt his dad's right hand come down on his arm.

'Stop,' Dad said.

Roy looked into his dad's eyes and smiled.

'You're speaking more,' Roy said quietly. His throat felt tight. He coughed.

Dad shook his head. 'Uh-uh,' he said.

Next Roy felt his dad's right hand grip Roy's right hand. It was a firm grip. Almost painful. But that was fine with Roy: in fact, he wanted it to hurt more. He wanted to feel the grip tighten even more, because he needed to know that – even though he was half-paralysed and could barely manage a word a week – his dad was strong.

'I'm really happy you'll be there today,' Roy said.

'Mmm,' Dad half-smiled.

'I'm going to score a goal for you,' Roy stared at his dad. 'I promise.'

Dad winked and Roy felt all the tension, stress and anxiety in his body lift. He felt strong. As strong as his dad's grip. He would take that with him into the game.

Roy's mum drove them to the ground. It was three hours before kick-off when they pulled up into one of the parking spaces the club reserved for disabled supporters.

Roy and Rocky helped Dad out of the car and into his wheelchair. What used to take twenty minutes now took five. They were getting good at this now.

And Dad was better than he'd ever been since his operation. Things were finally looking up for the Race family.

Roy wheeled Dad through the car park to the main reception of Mel Park, where the rest of his family were going to have a meal while he prepared for the game. The sun was beating down on them: it was a lovely day. The pitch would be firm, Roy thought. No mud. No uneven bounces like he used to have playing for Grimroyd on the Moor. Roy felt optimistic. And strong too, after his heart to heart with Dad the night before.

Several fans stopped to shake Dad's hand and clap Roy on the back.

'You must be proud of your lad, Danny?'

'Mmm.'

'Good to see you, Mr Race. And good luck, Roy.'

'Thanks.'

Staff from the club – including stewards – came over to say hello.

Everything was looking good.

'This is the most important day of my

life, Dad,' Roy said, when they were alone and in the shade of the main stand.

'Mmm.'

Dad bent his right arm back and clasped Roy's hand again. Roy liked it. That firm grip. It felt like love to Roy. Something he needed.

'F...' Dad said.

'What Dad?' Roy was desperate for another word from his dad. One, because it meant his dad was speaking more. Two, because he knew any word Dad managed to get out was an important word.

'Ff...'

Dad was pointing. Roy followed his arm. And there was Ffion.

She always seemed to appear like this, out of nowhere, forever seeing Roy before he saw her.

Roy studied her face. She was smiling. A good sign.

'Hi, Mr Race,' Ffion said, bending down to give Roy's dad a kiss on the cheek.

'Mmm.'

'Roy?'

'Ffion?'

The two sixteen-year-olds smiled at each other.

'I wanted to see you before the match,' Ffion said, loosening her Melchester Rovers scarf. 'To say you were right. That stuff you wouldn't tell me. You did the right thing.'

Roy felt his shoulders and chest relax.

'Thanks,' he said.

'And I shouldn't have asked you.'

Roy shook his head. 'You were doing it for the club.'

'So were you.'

They both laughed.

'Let me make it up to you,' Ffion said.

Roy swallowed. 'Okay then,' he said.

Ffion smiled. 'How?'

'Come to France with me,' Roy blurted out.

Ffion looked stunned. She stepped back. Roy thought he heard her gasp.

'Me and Rocky,' Roy said quickly, worried she'd taken what he'd said the wrong way. 'Look, Hugo's given us – well, you – a thank you for helping him. Tickets, flights and hotels for the World Cup next month. All on him.'

'No.'

Roy smiled. 'Yes.'

'We can't accept that.'

'We can,' Roy said. 'He'd be upset if we didn't.'

Ffion was grinning. And Roy suddenly felt a bit better. Whatever happened in this match – win or lose – he still had that to look forward to. Then he chastised himself.

There could be only one result.

A win.

They had to win.

25

THE NOISE AS Melchester Rovers ran out onto the pitch was unbelievable. A roar. A roar that Roy had never heard before, but somehow recognised.

Roy's dad had told him about it. More than quarter of a century ago when Mel Park was always full and the fans were celebrating trophy after trophy, making history, there had been a wall of noise from the home fans. A noise with a name.

The Rovers Roar. That's what Roy was hearing.

And it meant Melchester Rovers were back.

History waiting to be made again.

Melchester versus Kingsbay – the first leg of the League Two play-off semi-final – began just like the other two games they'd played against Kingsbay this season.

Brutally.

Every challenge from the opposition was just that little bit harder than it needed to be.

The visitor's centre forward was doing his best to knock Lofty Peak into next week and had also put his shoulder through Gordon Stewart after an early corner. But Dan Paconowski was all over them if they did. Not as tall as Lofty, he looked twice as tough and the Kingsbay players were backing off from him.

Roy was shoved over in the tenth minute. No free kick given.

The same defender came in to shoulder him off the ball soon after, but this time Roy pushed back, like Coach had insisted, using his body weight to hold the player off and turn to play Paco Diaz down the left. Paco avoided an ugly lunge and skipped on to put in a cross that ricocheted off a defender and out of Blackie Gray's range.

Blackie was hacked to the ground, but he jumped straight back up.

Vic Guthrie was bundled into some advertising boards. Paco was there in seconds to lift him to his feet.

Roy grinned. The training they'd done to cope with Kingsbay's physicality, their size advantage, their cynicism. It had worked. Melchester were not overawed: they had learned. And the teamwork too. It was there. And it was beginning pay off.

Melchester forced attack after attack as the momentum of the game swung their way. They already had three shots on target before Vic broke free from a scything tackle and played the ball forward to Paco Diaz's feet.

Twenty-seven minutes on the clock.

Paco took the ball, turned, stepped over it and suddenly the three defenders between him and the goal had vanished.

Roy took two steps to the side, unsettling

his marker, then sprinted at an angle towards the penalty area. With two giant defenders closing him down, Roy felt a twinge of fear. The injury he'd had. That came from an ugly foul from behind. He sensed the pain and fear he'd felt when he'd been put out of the game for weeks. Just for a split second. But, instead of giving in to that fear, Roy ran harder, using all of his youthful pace to beat the heavier, older opposition players.

He had ten yards on the defenders when Paco's ball rolled perfectly into his path, the keeper advancing on him, narrowing the angles.

Roy touched it lightly, sensed Blackie making a supporting run to his left, played it to Blackie, then moved hard to his right, expecting Blackie to roll the ball across the area to give Roy an open goal.

Blackie did exactly what Roy knew he

would do, falling as he lost his balance, but delivering a perfect pass.

The Kingsbay keeper did his best to intercept the pass, sticking his leg out, but Roy had it, slid in, made contact and watched as the ball spun into the bottom right corner of the net.

The noise was deafening.

The surge of adrenaline in Roy was overwhelming. Tears in his eyes, he scrambled past his teammates and fell at his dad's feet. Twenty thousand watched Roy hug his Dad, then turn to high-five his best mate, Blackie Gray.

It was the stuff of dreams.

MELCHESTER ROVERS WENT into the dressing rooms at half time buzzing.

Melchester Rovers 1 – 0 Kingsbay.

They weren't being bullied.

They were running Kingsbay off the park.

Roy came into the dressing room last, allowing Blackie to put his arm around him as they left the pitch.

'Twisted my knee,' Blackie grimaced. 'Setting up your goal.'

Johnny Dexter saw them both and took Blackie off Roy's hands.

'Nolan,' Johnny said, 'get warmed up outside. You're coming on for Blackie.'

Roy noticed Johnny glance across at Mighty Mouse who was sitting on the physio's table puffing his cheeks. Johnny narrowed his eyes as he studied the boss. Roy looked at Mouse now: he looked the most exhausted of them all, even though he'd been sat in the dugout for the last forty-five minutes.

'Roy, get me some ice for Blackie's knee,' Coach said. 'Mouse is feeling a bit off colour. I'll give the team talk.'

THERE WAS SOMETHING wrong as Roy and his teammates jogged on to the pitch for the second half. The Rovers Roar wasn't as loud as it had been in the first half. Something had changed. Something important.

Was it Blackie's injured knee? Mouse being unwell? Was it having a team talk from Johnny, not Mouse?

Roy had no idea.

Three minutes into the second half Kingsbay won a corner. Vic was in among his players, geeing them up. Focusing on the defensive quartet of Duncan, Dan, Lofty and Asif.

'Fight for the ball,' he shouted. 'Remember training. Win that ball!'

Kingsbay's winger took the corner and – without another player touching it – the ball cannoned off the Melchester Rovers bar.

The crowd gasped.

There was fear in the stands now. Fear on the pitch.

Suddenly – with the home crossbar struck – Rovers' fans were more worried about conceding than trying to score. The players too.

Kingsbay had smelled blood.

But, still, Roy pushed forward every time Melchester attacked, running alongside Patrick Nolan. But, every time Roy got the ball into Nolan's feet, Nolan scuffed it or showed too much of it to a Kingsbay player.

Then possession was lost again.

It was frustrating. It was infuriating.

It knocked the confidence of the young Melchester Rovers team. Every move they made led to nothing because Patrick's touch was off.

Then, with twenty minutes to go, Patrick gave it away one too many times, and Kingsbay were onto the stray ball like a pack of wolves going for the kill

Roy tracked back as fast as he could, overtaking Lofty as three, then four, Kingsbay players took on two Melchester defenders.

It was Vernon Elliott who committed the foul. Twenty yards out.

Immediately Elliott was up on his feet. 'Ref! I got the ball! Come on...'

The ref frowned and pulled out a yellow card.

'Arguing with the ref, son. Keep a lid on it.'

Roy shook his head as he watched Vic setting up a wall with a worried look on his face. He remembered training, and the strong possibility that Kingsbay might score from free kicks like this. One of the Kingsbay forwards strolled forward with the ball under his arm. He was chatting to a teammate, laughing as he placed the ball down on the grass. Another exchange of words. Another laugh. Then the referee's whistle.

Kingsbay's number ten set up to take it,

but instead of striking the ball towards the goal, fooling everyone and tapped it a metre to the side for Kingsbay's main striker Phil Earle to hit it.

Hard.

Hard and fast and straight.

The free kick smashed through the wall, bounced off the crossbar – and into the net.

Goal.

Melchester Rovers 1 – 1 Kingsbay.

The noise in the stadium was all coming from the away end now.

Roy felt like he'd been punched in the stomach.

'Come on. Let's get this back,' he heard Vic shouting above the noise of the Kingsbay fans. Roy clapped his hands to echo his captain's call.

As the match wore on, Roy was drawn deeper and deeper into the game, eventually finding himself all the way back at the edge of his own penalty area. Kingsbay's power and strength were overwhelming now. The game felt – to Roy – as if it was boys against men. That was the phrase Johnny had used back in those first few games they'd played in the autumn when most of the Rovers squad weren't even seventeen. Roy was suddenly relieved this was a two-legged game. They could never play this badly again, even if the next leg *was* at Kingsbay's ground.

But this game still had to play out: there was more drama to come.

A long throw from Kingsbay into the Melchester penalty area.

'Everybody back,' Roy heard Vic shout. 'Nolan. You stay out. Hold the ball up if it comes to you.'

Roy stood with Vic, each of them marking a Kingsbay striker.

The ball came in high, skimmed off a Kingsbay shoulder, Roy and Vic and the two opposition strikers jumping at once, as Gordon Stewart raced out to punch the ball clear.

Roy would go over what happened next a thousand times. Probably more. Trying to make sense of it. He'd felt himself fall, tumbling into Vic and two Kingsbay players. A heap on bodies on the floor. The ball coming at them. Then the ball hitting one of them – Roy had no idea who, but it wasn't him – and ricocheting out behind the goal.

Roy heard the referee's whistle. He stared over at the ref to see what he'd decided. His heart dropped in his chest as he realised that the referee was pointing at the spot.

Roy shouted, getting to his feet, then helping Vic up too. 'No! Ref!? No!'

The Kingsbay fans were cheering like they'd won promotion already.

And now the referee was beckoning Roy over.

Roy pointed to himself, questioning the referee.

The referee nodded, a severe look on his face.

Roy jogged over to him, keeping his eyes on the ground, trying to work out what the

referee had seen. Or maybe it wasn't what he'd seen: it was what he'd heard. Roy shouting out to disagree with the penalty decision. If only he'd kept his mouth shut. He was going to get a yellow, like Vernon. He'd never been booked in his whole time playing football. He approached the referee and looked up to see a chaos of colour all around him, a cacophony of noise, then a huge boo coming from three sides of the ground. The Melchester fans were unhappy. About something else now.

But what?

When Roy looked up he understood.

The referee was holding up a card to Roy. A red card.

'What? Ref? Why? I don't...'

'Handball preventing a goal, son. You need to leave the pitch. Now.'

'CATASTROPHIC. DEFEAT WOULD be catastrophic.'

As Roy walked off the pitch, head down, crushed, Johnny Dexter's words echoed round his head.

Catastrophic.

The booing around him was deafening. Louder than the Rovers Roar. Roy felt hands on his back, comfort from his team mates. He glanced up and saw Vic Guthrie, pink-faced, his eyes bloodshot, staring at him, mouth gaping open.

He looked furious.

Roy didn't want to look at anyone. Not

the players. Not the fans as he came closer and closer to them pitch side. Were they booing him? Or the referee?

Maybe it was him. Why not? He'd just been sent off with a straight red. That meant Melchester were down to ten men. And that Roy would miss the next game. *And* they would probably be going into the second leg 2-1 down if the penalty went in.

So they must be booing him. If they thought he'd handballed it.

But he hadn't. Roy was sure he had not touched the ball with his hand. It had to have been someone else. Surely he would have felt it.

Reaching the edge of the pitch he heard voices from the crowd. 'Idiot... what were you thinking?'

Roy stared into the crowd and shook his head. 'Not me,' he shouted. 'It wasn't me.'

But all eyes were on the penalty area now. Roy could tell by the drop in volume – and the whistles from the Tom Tully stand – that it was about to come.

Then he saw his dad in the disabled seating area.

Roy crouched on his knees next to his dad. He looked into his dad's eyes.

'It wasn't me, Dad.'

A blast on the whistle.

His dad shook his head and put his hand on Roy's arm.

Then the away end exploded with noise. A noise that was drowned out by more booing from around Mel Park.

Melchester Rovers 1 – 2 Kingsbay.

And at that moment Roy's world fell in. Because he knew – if it really had been him that had given away the penalty – that he'd just killed Melchester Rovers.

THE STORY CONTINUES!

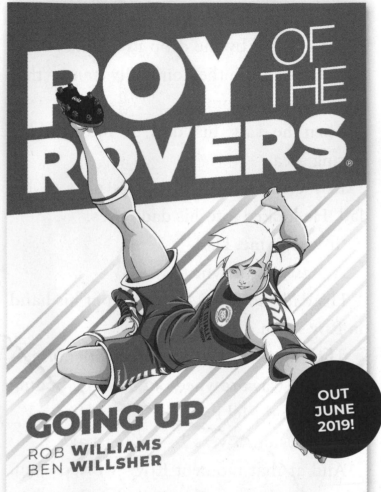

ROY OF THE ROVERS®

GOING UP

ROB WILLIAMS
BEN WILLSHER

OUT JUNE 2019!

The end of the season is here – but is this the end of the dream, too? If Rovers don't win promotion, it's all over. Can Roy save the club he's loved all his life? Find out in **GOING UP**, the awesome new graphic novel out in June 2019!

For more **ROY OF THE ROVERS** follow us online:

www.royoftheroversofficial.com

ROY OF THE ROVERS GOES DIGITAL!

Roy of the Rovers is back, with brand new comics and books starring Roy Race and the mighty Melchester Rovers – and now you can keep up to date with all things Roy on your smartphone or tablet!

Through the new *Roy of the Rovers* app, you'll be able to read the awesome new stories, grab some free comics, and even play Rovers-themed word games!

SEARCH FOR *ROY OF THE ROVERS* IN YOUR APP STORE OF CHOICE!

ROY OF THE ROVERS

THE FIRST SEASON

Keep track of every new **Roy of the Rovers** book here!
Don't forget to tick the boxes as you read each one.

FICTION

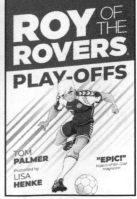

BOOK 1	BOOK 2	BOOK 3
SCOUTED	**TEAMWORK**	**PLAY-OFFS**

Author: Tom Palmer
Out: October 2018
ISBN: 978-1-78108-698-8

Author: Tom Palmer
Out: February 2019
ISBN: 978-1-78108-707-7

Author: Tom Palmer
Out: May 2019
ISBN: 978-1-78108-722-0

Roy Race is the most talented striker in Melchester – but is he good enough to catch the eye of the Melchester Rovers scouts?

Life gets tricky for Roy as he adjusts to life in the spotlight. Fortune and glory await, but can Roy juggle football, fame and family?

Crunch time for Rovers: the end of the season is here, the club is in deep trouble, and it's down to Roy to bring a bit of hope back to the Melchester faithful.

READD?   **READ?**   **READ?**

COMICS

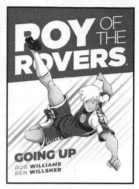

BOOK 1	BOOK 2	BOOK 3
KICK-OFF	**FOUL PLAY**	**GOING UP**

Writer: Rob Williams
Artist: Ben Willsher
Out: November 2018
ISBN: 978-1-78108-652-0

Writer: Rob Williams
Artist: Ben Willsher
Out: March 2019
ISBN: 978-1-78108-669-8

Writer: Rob Williams
Artist: Ben Willsher
Out: June 2019
ISBN: 978-1-78108-673-5

Roy Race is 16, talented, and desperate to make it as a footballer. But is he good enough for Melchester Rovers? Now's the time to prove if he's got what it takes to become Roy of the Rovers.

Roy picks up an injury that puts him on the sidelines, and suddenly there's competition for his place as a brand new - and brilliant - striker is brought in by the management...

Roy and the team have battled through a tough season, but have they got enough left to get promoted? Or will they fall at the final hurdle and see the club sold by its greedy owner?

READ? ☐   **READ?** ☐   **READ?** ☐

THE OFFICIAL MELCHESTER ROVERS HOME KIT 2018/19 IS OUT NOW!

Show your support for *Roy of the Rovers* with the official home kit of the mighty Melchester Rovers!

Look the part, just like Roy! Designed by Hummel in the iconic Rovers red and yellow, this is a shirt every Melchester fan - and every aspiring Roy Race - can be proud to wear!

Featuring:
- **Embroidered Melchester Rovers badge**
- **Classic Melchester Rovers red and yellow colours**
- **Iconic Hummel chevron design**
- **Made from lightweight performance material**

AVAILABLE NOW ONLY FROM THE OFFICIAL *ROY OF THE ROVERS* SHOP AT:

www.royoftheroversofficial.com